Venice Actually
a hot holiday novella

Kelly Reynolds

Contents

Author's Note

Venice Actually is the second book in Holidays in LA series, though it can be read as a standalone. This low angst, high heat romance novella between a pansexual, mid-size woman and her dirty-talking, anxious Brit, takes place between Thanksgiving and New Year's Eve.

Please be advised that this book is an **open-door** romance, meaning there is **on-page, explicit** sexual content (between consenting adults), including oral sex, vaginal sex, anal play, spanking (in a variety of ways), shower play, and bondage. There's also recreational use of alcohol and marijuana, discussions about anxiety, discussions about fatphobia, an on-the-page anxiety attack, PCOS rep, menstruation, family/generational trauma, grief, and mention of the death of a parent. Mature readers only.

Sidenote, if you *must* have shower sex, please use lube.

Lots of lube.

For all of the oldest/only children,
whose independence scares the shit out of their families.

They might not understand you,
but that doesn't make you wrong.

Keep doing you, babes.

Chapter One

November 28th

Leighton

"What kind of Dickensian villain evicts someone on Thanksgiving?" The *clack-clack* of my favorite heeled boots on the pavement gave rhythm to my fury.

"I know you're pissed, Leigh," Nora offered, "but please don't take it out on those beautiful boots." She whipped her violet-colored curls over her shoulder and handed me the tray of cheddar biscuits. Gammy Wheatley's famous recipe. The one my mom had dictated to me over the phone, step-by-step, for two hours yesterday because it was "easier" than sending a link or screenshot. "You promised me I could borrow them for my work party next week."

Even though Nora, my boss-slash-best friend's girlfriend, had a good four or five inches on me, we'd learned early on in our friendship that we shared the same shoe size. Though why she, the star of Hulu's hit "space opera" *Andromeda 8,* wanted to borrow anything from me, a fashion design school dropout from Ohio, was beyond me.

"Don't worry," I told her, huffing out a breath. "I'll buff and shine them to your heart's content."

"No buffing necessary. Just slow down, will you?"

I did her one better and stopped completely. "Better?"

She rolled her eyes. "Much."

Was I acting like a petulant toddler? Sure. But in my defense, November had been one hell of a shitstorm. Quite literally.

November 5th, clogged toilet.

November 12th, clogged again.

November 21st, burst pipe because of, you guessed it, a clogged toilet. My roommates and I had woken to find an inch of water (and who knew what else) flooding the entire third floor.

Rather than make the necessary repairs, the landlord had taken the easy way out and sold the entire building to an ex-husband-and-wife house-flipping duo known best for their short-lived HGTV show and their even shorter marriage. Their vows might not have lasted, but they had certainly made a career out of exploiting LA's most historic buildings, not to mention the tenants—yours truly included—who lived there.

People paid top dollar for gentrification these days.

But the holiday cheer didn't end there.

As it turned out, it *could* get worse than shitty water and HGTV stars. Five days ago, I'd woken up to an empty apartment (because of course, my roommates had stranded me to spend Thanksgiving with their respective families) and an eviction notice duct-taped to our front door. I'd spent the rest of the day binge-watching all ten *Fast &*
Furious movies while stress-eating egg rolls and cookie dough.

Happy Turduck-ing Thanksgiving.

That led to here and now, me, stomping in a pair of boots I could barely afford outside of Bowie and Nora's house, an adorable bungalow that made the cottage from *The Holiday* look like a dilapidated shack. It was amazing how far we'd come in a year, some of us more so than others.

After a year of dating, Nora and Bowie had recently decided to take the elusive "next step"—the one I'd *heard* so much about, but had never experienced myself—and move in together. Like Nora and Bowie, most folks I knew were currently swimming in monogamous bliss, or so their Instagram feeds would have you believe. I, on the other hand, had spent the better half of my twenties actively avoiding *Cohabitation Station*, instead frequenting such stops as *Casual City* and *Situationship Square*. They'd seemed fun at the time and while I still enjoyed the occasional visit, now that I was in my thirties, I rode the "train" a lot less frequently, so to speak. I hadn't so much as seen a sign for *Cohabitation Station* in years.

But my best friend and his bombshell of a girlfriend were deliriously happy, and maybe that would be enough to get me through the holiday season. It's the most romantic, hectic, gut-wrenchingly lonely time of year.

I think that's how the song goes . . .

"Look, about your place," Nora said, hefting the case of wine I'd offered to pick up on my way to the party higher on her hips. "You can stay with us. So long as you don't mind the dog and a few . . . dozen boxes."

"Right, because there's nothing quite like sharing the 'honeymooning' phase with your boyfriend's coworker."

"You know you're more than just a coworker."

Nora was right, and I knew that. I'd worked for Bowie, alongside him, really, since he'd taken over his grandmother's tea shop nearly four years ago. At the time, he'd been fresh off the plane from England, and we'd bonded over both of us being so far from home. I'd shown him where to get the best tacos in town—a nondescript truck in Silverlake that only opened after dark—and he'd shared his gran's secret scone recipe. From what he told me, I was the only other person alive who knew it.

In short, Bowie was the brother I never knew I wanted.

"Maybe you could take a trip somewhere, recharge your batteries?"

"I love your boyfriend, but he doesn't exactly pay me enough for that," I told her.

"Gotcha."

What I didn't tell her was that I'd already begun looking for a new job. It wasn't that I didn't love working for my best friend. Of course, I did. But I also hadn't budgeted for an unexpected move right before the holidays, the most inconvenient and expensive time of year.

"Here's a thought," Nora mused. "You could always go home for the holidays. How long has it been since you've been back to—"

"No," I snapped, stopping Nora in her tracks. Her confusion wasn't lost on me. I might speak fluent sarcasm, but I didn't typically pop off on the people I cared about, except for that one time Bowie told me he didn't like Jack Black movies. If there was one thing I would *not* abide, it was Jack Black slander.

I took a deep breath—*God, those biscuits smell great*—to recenter myself. Nora and I might have grown closer since she and Bowie got together last Christmas, but she knew next to nothing about my family, and even less about my life B.L.A.—Before Los Angeles. Even Bowie didn't know much beyond the basics: born and raised in Ohio, oldest of two girls, left home at eighteen to pursue fashion design. And it was pretty obvious how *that* had turned out.

"Sorry," I said, softening my voice. "Home is *not* an option and the last thing I want to do is intrude on anybody's Christmas." She opened her mouth, probably to tell me that I wouldn't be intruding, that I was always welcome, blah blah blah. But before she could, I added, "I appreciate the offer, but the holidays are different. Besides, aren't you hosting Bowie's moms?"

She nibbled on her bottom lip. "Yeah, but . . ."

"Don't worry," I said, faking my best smile. "I'll figure it out." I picked up my pace. Maybe she wouldn't notice the quiver of my lips if I stayed a few feet ahead. "I always do."

It took one hour, two glasses of Cab, and three biscuits (okay, four) to take the edge off. And even then, I could still feel the walls closing in.

I was surrounded by people in love.

Nora and Bowie. Riley and Devin. Kendall and Peter.

It seemed like everywhere I turned, there were couples. Or, in the case of our coworker Hillary and her partners, throuples. That was right. I couldn't find anyone (emphasis on "one") to spend the holidays with, but Hillary had two people to love her. One might assume that being pansexual would broaden my options, but alas, not so much.

It seemed that Banger, Bowie's well-loved dachshund, and I were the only ones flying solo tonight.

"Alright, everybody! It's time for Scattergories," Nora's ex-room-mate, Riley, called from the opposite end of the room. I'd only met Riley a handful of times, but describing her as the "life of the party" would be an insult to both her and parties. Her energy knew no bounds. More importantly, judging by the way her spouse, Devin, never took their eyes off her, Riley was *their* life, with or without the party.

"You guys go on ahead," I said, waving them off. "I'm going to step out to smoke."

"You sure?" Nora asked. She was already in the midst of helping Riley pass out pens and paper to the rest of the group. Long gone were the days of King's Cup and Jell-O shots; thirty-somethings played board games and sipped red wine. All before eleven p.m.

"We're happy to wait for you," Bowie added from right beside me.

"Please don't," I said, smiling sweetly. I leaned in so only he could hear me. "I love you both, but I draw the line at Scattergories."

"It's good to know your love is conditional."

"We all have our dealbreakers, Bo. And mine is word games." I handed him my empty wine glass. "Please make sure this is full when I get back."

He snorted and nodded his head toward the back door. "The porch light is out, so watch your step."

I patted his shoulder, careful so as not to spill his wine, and made my way out onto the patio. It was a small space, tiny really, but any outdoor space was a rare find in an urban jungle like Los Angeles. I shut the door behind me and reached for the "emergency joint" in my jacket pocket for social occasions just like this. A glass or two of red might get me through Scattergories, but I'd need something stronger for whatever else Riley undoubtedly had planned. I was willing to risk the red (and green) hangover.

'Tis the season, after all.

I smoothed the tip of the paper before tucking it between my lips. I resisted the urge to look around to make sure nobody was watching. This was California, not Ohio, but old habits died hard. Even after a decade. Using my dollar store Bic lighter, I lit the fat end and sucked.

Deep. Until a familiar burn tickled my throat. Only then, did I tilt my head back and exhale.

"Fancy seeing you here."

Killian

I'd never owned a cat or any pet, really—the life of a professional footballer didn't allow for much beyond eating, sleeping, and rigorous training—but based on the Tiktok videos I'd seen after I'd (somehow) stumbled onto #CatTok last year, I couldn't help but compare the way that Leighton recoiled to the way a cat might respond when unexpectedly faced with bath water.

Apparently, just the timbre of my voice was enough to set her off. And why did that turn me on? Oh, that's right . . .

Because I was in love with Leighton Wheatley.

I knew it. My best mate, Bowie, knew it, which meant he'd probably told Nora. Hell, for all I knew, Leighton knew, too. Not that I'd ever be the one to tell her. My anxiety would never allow such a thing. It took two weeks just to mentally prepare myself for tonight's festivities, and even then, it hadn't done much good. I'd spent most of the evening alone on the patio.

With her shoulders hunched near to her ears, she pivoted to face me. Truly, it was a wonder she hadn't seen me in the first place, but I blamed that on the lack of lighting. At six-foot-two, I didn't exactly blend in. Then again, I wasn't in Leeds anymore. This was Hollywood, land of the free . . . gift with purchase, home of the *Greys* (*Anatomy* or *Fifty Shades of*, take your pick). Out here, tall, burly men were a dime a dozen.

Forgoing her usual sarcastic response, she took another hit of the joint. That didn't bother me. On the contrary, it gave me ample time to admire her, to catalogue every beautiful detail from the top of her wavy brown locks to the heels of her ass-kicking boots. *Bad idea, mate. Now you're thinking about her ass.* And what an ass it was. Thick, luscious. *Edible.* Hypothetically speaking, of course. I'd need some . . . quality time alone with said ass to test that theory. The best "evidence" I had to go off was a lone memory of her in a bikini during a camping trip we'd taken with Bowie and Nora.

A memory I'd wanked off to on more than one occasion.

"Siri, play 'Creep' by Radiohead."

Everything about Leighton Wheatley wrecked me. Even now, a year after we'd met, I still couldn't put my finger on what had first drawn me to her. But believe me when I say, I'd love nothing more than to soak my fingers in all things Leighton Wheatley.

Here she was, juicy pink lips wrapped around a joint—something I hadn't indulged in since well before my days at uni—and all I could picture was her on her knees, lips wrapped around my greedy cock, sucking every vestige of life from me. And I'd be all too happy to give it to her. Every last drop.

Well, there's some new wank material for you, pervert.

Ironically, it was the cloud of smoke drifting from her lips that pulled me out of my lust-induced fog.

"Killjoy." I felt the corner of my lips kick up. Sexy *and* sassy.

"Leia."

The adorable ridge between her brows furrowed. Never had a frown turned me on and yet, I could already feel my trousers tightening.

"I should've known *you'd* be here."

"Here on the dark patio?" She rolled her eyes. We'd been playing this game for going on a year—the one where she mistook my love and adoration for a playground crush's teases and taunts, and I did my best not to throw up in her presence—and damn if I didn't love it.

"Looking forward to the holidays?"

Such a wanker. Want to ask her about her favorite color next?

"Oh, absolutely," she scoffed before snubbing out the end of her joint. She tucked what was left of it back into her jacket pocket and kept her hands there. We were having an unseasonably chilly (not cold, *chilly*) autumn this year. At least that was what the locals told me. It felt like any old, dreary day in England to me.

"Any big plans?"

"Hmmm, let's see. I can't decide what I'm more excited for." The edge to her voice told me I'd inadvertently hit a nerve. "Looking for a new apartment, even though nobody is renting at this time of year, or looking for a new job so I can afford the new apartment I can't seem to find. What do you think?"

And just like that, the game was over. I might do a lousy job of hiding my feelings, but I certainly didn't play when it came to hers.

"Sorry, what's going on?"

"You heard me." She turned toward the door, but I wasn't letting her get away that easily. This conversation was far from over.

"Leighton." I didn't know if it was the exceptionally deep tone of voice or the fact that I'd used her actual name, but in either case, it was enough to halt her movement just inches from the door. "What's happened?"

She quickly explained her situation, all while avoiding my gaze and nervously wringing her hands together. Using her hands when she talks was reason number fifty-two why I loved Leighton.

Yes, there was a list.

No, I hadn't written it down. Because *that* would be *too* creepy. At least, that was how I justified it to myself.

From the time we'd spent together over the last year (always with friends, never alone), she'd made it more than clear that she wasn't one to share her worries or insecurities. With anyone. To be fair, I hadn't exactly made it clear that I was interested in hearing them either. So, the fact that she was sharing them now, with me of all people, spoke volumes.

By the time she finished, I felt nearly as gutted as she looked. The way I wanted to wrap my arms around this woman, even as she shifted her eyes between me and the door, clearly calculating how long it would take to make a swift exit.

Reason #12: She's an independent problem-solver.

I wanted to help solve her problems. Preferably while she braided my hair while we watched *Murder, She Wrote* together. Naked. A guy could dream.

Even now, I was busy running scenarios in my head. That was an unfortunate side effect of being an athlete, a neurodivergent athlete at that. Forget the fact that I could never turn my brain off, even when it came to matters of the heart. Regardless of whether I was on or off the field, I had a habit of visualizing the "play," as well as all the potential outcomes.

For instance, Scenario A: I offer Leighton the money she needs to find a new apartment. I ruled this one out almost immediately. Leighton wasn't a person who readily accepted help from others, so it was almost impossible to imagine her accepting financial aid of any kind.

Scenario B: I buy back her apartment from the *shite* landlord. Although, thinking on it, I'd probably have to buy the whole building.

I could afford it, sure. But if a few thousand dollars were likely to piss Leighton off, lord knows a few million would put her over the edge.

Scenario C had something to do with dogs and a mall Santa – again, I wish I understood how my brain worked. Moving on.

That brought me to Scenario D. *Well, I've got nothing to lose . . .*

"Move in with me."

"You've got to be kidding me."

"Not at all." I grinned "I've got the room. More than enough. Hell, bring Lolo and Hector, too. I've got enough spare rooms for all of you."

"You remember my roommates' names? Didn't you only meet them like once or twice?"

"Um, yeah."

It was three times, actually. Once at the tearoom where she and Bowie worked, once outside of Nora and Bowie's house, and the last time during a mini golf fundraiser that Bowie had all but dragged me to. I'd played the worst round of mini golf that evening, mostly because I'd spent the entire time watching Leighton laugh and play with her friends. But she didn't need to know that.

She snorted. "Well, I appreciate the offer, Richie Rich, but they're all set. They've got . . . *families* to spend the holidays with."

Judging by the way she practically choked on the word, I knew there was more to that story.

"So, just us then?" *Settle down, boy.*

"I guess. Where do you live anyway?"

Wait. Was she really considering my offer? I tried to contain my earnestness when I replied, "Venice."

"Venice?! Geez, could you be any farther away?"

"It's not Venice, Italy."

"I work in Silver Lake, so it might as well be." She wasn't wrong. I had it on good authority that the Los Angeles highway system *was* the sixth circle of Hell. And according to Nora, a born and raised Los Angeleno, the local dating scene was the seventh. She'd explained it all to me over tea after the stylist I'd been dating who lived in Echo Park dumped me for being "geographically undesirable."

I worked in the South Bay, so it made sense to live on the west side of town. But I knew that most people, Leighton included, couldn't afford that luxury. Hell, it took years of bruises, broken bones, and sleepless nights for me to be able to afford it.

"I don't know," she murmured, tucking her hands back into her pockets. She was closing in on herself, a feeling I knew all too well. "I doubt I can afford a place in Venice anyways."

"I'm sure we can work something out." It took about two seconds for me to realize how that sounded. This wasn't *Pretty Woman*. I wasn't Richard Gere. I could feel the color draining from my face. Thank God it was dark out. "That's not . . . I would never."

"Relax, Sherlock," she said, rolling her eyes. She shifted from one foot to another.

When she looked back toward the house, I surreptitiously rubbed my palms down my thighs one, two, three times before starting again. "I only meant that whatever you were thinking before, you should know that you're *not* out of options. And if you insist on paying rent, even though I don't need it, you can just pay me what you did for your apartment."

I waited with bated breath. Maybe I should've run more scenarios before offering up a room in my house, but—

"Okay."

Wait, did she just . . .

"Okay, I'll stay. But it's only because you're literally my last option, *and* it's too late to find anyplace else affordable before Christmas, *and* there's no way in hell I'm asking my family for money, *and—"*

"You could've just left it at 'okay.'"

She bit back a smile. *Glad to know we're getting somewhere, Leia.*

Just then, a cheer erupted from inside the house, drawing our attention. I stepped around her to open the door, bringing us almost front-to-front. Being this close to her truly emphasized the differences between us. Where I was tall and bulky, even after nearly two years of retirement from football, she was shorter and plush. In all the right places. Plenty to grab onto and never let go. That was my plan at least.

"Shall we?" I asked, gesturing for her to enter the house. She stepped in and I followed. It didn't take long to find the source of commotion. From what I could tell, Riley and Nora were busy arguing over whether vibrators were in fact "bad habits."

Leighton and I hung back from the rest of the crowd. Her leaning against the sideboard, where Kacey Musgraves was currently belting out Christmas hits from Nora and Bowie's turntable, and me two steps behind her. Just how I preferred it. After a minute or two, she blinked up at me and pursed her lips. "You know, I doubt my rent would pay the electric bill at your place, killjoy."

"That's not a problem." And then in a surprising moment of confidence, I leaned in until I was close enough to smell the weed and wildflowers (a deadly combination) emanating off her skin and whispered, "Just so long as it covers the pool maintenance."

"Pool?!"

Every pair of eyes turned our way. Leighton smiled awkwardly, her cheeks reddening to the color of Bowie's hair, before launching into explanations. While she answered questions and I avoided eye contact with my best friend, the man who probably knew both Leighton and I better than anyone, my latest scenario began to play out in my head.

The one where I made Leighton Wheatley mine by Christmas.

Chapter Two

December 3rd

Leighton

"Alright." Janelle huffed. I could almost picture her curling up on the couch, a pillow in her lap. "Run me through it one more time."

I flopped down on my bedroom floor, alongside the box full of crochet supplies I'd been packing when my sister called. Nora and Devin would be back any second with more boxes, and I was still nowhere near done with my closet. I'd greatly underestimated the amount of crap I owned.

"Look, it's a place to stay," I told her, cradling the phone to my ear while I rifled through the box beside me. "He's just a friend of a friend."

"Mm-kay." Her doubt rang clearly through the phone, even though she was nearly two-thousand miles away.

"It's true. I can barely stand the guy."

"This is the soccer player, right?"

"Retired, but yes." From what Bowie had told me, and after doing some light social media stalking of my own, I knew that Killian had had, by all accounts, an illustrious professional soccer career. Unfortunately, that career had come to an impromptu end after a car accident a few years back.

But he'd bounced back almost immediately—why did everything always seem to work out for *some* people?—by landing himself a head coaching position with the South Bay Sounders, California's latest addition to the National Women's Soccer League. The fact that his best friend from childhood *also* lived in L.A. probably didn't hurt either.

"The one that looks like Thor but talks like Loki?"

"Yes," I said through gritted teeth. This time, I was the one huffing.

I had no qualms admitting that Killian was, to quote Derek Zoolander, "Really, really, ridiculously good-looking." From his chiseled physique to his impeccably well-coiffed beard, and, of course, the effortless way he tied his hair up. The man could teach classes on perfecting the messy bun.

But we didn't need to talk about it. I didn't need the reminder, from my sister of all people, that this man had *everything* going for him—the perfect house, the perfect career, the perfect body. And then, there was me. Unhoused, uneducated me, though, truth be told, I fucking *loved* my body. Every stretch mark, roll, and wayward hair. I'd be lying if I said it hadn't taken one hell of an emotional roller coaster ride to reach that point, but nevertheless, she persisted. Just because I loved my body didn't mean the world loved it, too. I knew well before my failed stint in fashion school that this world wasn't too kind to people with bodies like mine. And yet it *worshiped* people who looked like Killian. Especially when those people were athletes. With money. And Tom Hiddleston-like accents. Los Angeles was overrun with handsome Brits, as was my personal social circle.

So, sue me for having petty, superficial thoughts about him. When it came down to it, I was only trying to protect myself. I didn't know if I could stomach another hurt. *Another failure.*

"I know I'm your sister, but I can't say I blame you for wanting to spend Christmas with a hunky Brit over your own family."

"About that," I started. "Please don't tell Mom and Dad about this. I'd rather they not have any new . . . ammo to use against me."

"Oh, stop. They're not that bad." There was no stopping the laugh that escaped my mouth. "They're not!"

"That's because, sister of mine, we do not have the same parents."

"Now, we both know that's not true," she argued. Nellie had just finished law school and was currently waiting for the results of her Ohio state bar exam. If there was one thing my little sister knew how to do, it was argue. "Have you forgotten my fourteenth birthday?"

"Please, I've spent years trying to forget."

I'd been eighteen at the time. Our dad had decided my sister's *Camp Rock* themed sleepover was the perfect occasion to show a group of high school girls some home videos . . . of Janelle's and my births. Maybe not the ideal birth control method for teenagers, but it'd kept me from having sex until my mid-twenties.

"That's not what I meant, though." I lay back on the floor and kicked my legs up toward the wall. Talking to my sister about boys and our parents made me feel like a teenager again. "*My* parents question me if I breathe the wrong way. *Yours* support every single decision you make."

"Now, that's not true," she argued. She might make a world-class lawyer, but this was one case she didn't have a shot at winning. I went on.

"Every person you date."

"I'm sure there was somebody they didn't like," she mused.

"Every outfit, every haircut." And because I knew it would tick her off, I added, "Including that time you gave yourself baby bangs, which I know you know were awful. What did Mom say?"

"That I looked like a French film star."

I waved my hand in the air for emphasis. "Ladies and gentlemen of the jury, I rest my case."

"You know they mean well, though."

"Sure, I do." This wasn't the first time my sister and I had had this conversation. It wasn't the second, third, or fiftieth time either. "But I also know they've made it next to impossible for me to want to share anything about my life with them because it's never good enough."

Safe enough. Successful enough. The laundry list of ways I disappointed my parents lived rent-free in my head.

"But how will Mom know where to send your Christmas mouse?"

I rolled my eyes. Like many women of a certain age, our mother had an affinity for crafts. And Minnie Mouse. She was also a big believer in one-of-a-kind gifts, the more unique or homemade, the better. And thus, the "Christmas Mouse" was born. Nellie had barely been out of diapers when we received our first Christmas mice, hand-painted, ceramic rodents no bigger than the size of my palm that Mom made herself during her weekly pottery class. Some kids woke up to stockings full of candy on Christmas morning; Nellie and I got polka-dotted rats. And while individually, they didn't take up much room, together, they filled an empty Converse shoebox that lived permanently under my bed. Thankfully, I didn't see my parents visiting me anytime soon. Just the thought of displaying those mismatched critters for others to see gave me hives.

"Wow, you're right. Now I'm definitely not telling them that I moved."

"Lex Hawthorne."

"Who?" I asked, startled by the abrupt subject change.

"The boyfriend that Mom and Dad didn't like. Lex "Licks" Hawthorne, my date to junior prom. He had an earring."

"Huh."

"What? Surprised I dated someone they didn't approve of?"

"More like, surprised you dated someone called 'Licks.'"

My sister had always been the shy, introverted one—just one more reason for our parents to favor her—so the fact that she'd dated a guy nicknamed for, what I assumed, was his tongue game was surprising, to say the least.

"Let's just say his ear wasn't the only part that was pierced."

Well, damn.

That launched us into a fit of giggles. I was still lying on the floor, catching my breath, when Nora and Devin walked in.

"That doesn't look like packing your closet to me," Nora chastised.

I gestured to the phone still clutched in my hand. "I just hung up with my sister."

"Is your family going to come visit for the holidays?" Devin asked.

"Absolutely not."

Even from my spot upside down on the ground, I didn't miss the look they exchanged. The one that said, *"Do you want to ask her or should I?"*

"And before you ask, no, I don't want to talk about it. My family and I have a complicated relationship, so let's just leave it at that." I sat up a bit too quickly, the blood draining from my head. Once the floor stopped spinning, I added, "What I do want to do is finish packing so we can take a load over tonight. Sound good?"

"Sure," Nora said, drawing out the word. At the same time, Devin shrugged and said, "Whatever you want."

We spent the next couple of hours packing up almost a decade's worth of memories. It probably would've gone faster if we hadn't switched the background music selection from Nora's "Emo Songs of the 2000s" playlist to the *Six: The Musical* soundtrack.

As it turned out, Devin and I both had a thing for showtunes.

It was while I was putting the last of my bedding in a bag and belting out the final refrain of "Don't Lose Ur Head" when I heard the ruffle of papers behind me. "Did you draw these?" Devin asked.

My stomach dropped. Somehow, I knew what they were talking about even before I looked. There they were, standing by the open top drawer of a desk I'd found on Hollywood Blvd, holding my dusty design portfolio.

"Yup," I said, hoping they'd leave it at that.

"They're beautiful. I had no idea you were an artist."

I scoffed. Maybe at one point in time I'd considered myself an artist, but that day was long gone. Buried beneath a decade's worth of doubt and a lifetime of student debt.

Nora set aside the stack of books she'd just finished pulling from my bookcase and crossed the room to Devin's side. Her face lit up with equal parts shock and awe when she saw my sketches.

"Seriously, girl," she said, "these are gorgeous."

"They're nothing. Honestly, I don't even know why I've kept them this long."

"Because it would be a crime to toss them." Her eyes suddenly widened. *Rut-roh.* She snatched the open portfolio from Devin and turned it toward me. "Especially this one. Can you make this for me? Because I would pay good money for something to make my body look like *that.*"

I felt my lips kick up. The sketch in question was one of my favorites. A sleeveless knit sweaterdress that molded to the model's body like a second skin. I'd always envisioned creating clothes for bigger bodies like mine, but the idea to use knits had come later. During my junior year of high school, I'd developed a bad case of pneumonia and had to spend almost a month at home, in bed. I was desperate for a hobby, something, anything other than more episodes of *Jersey Shore*, to keep me entertained. So, I took up knitting. And crocheting. And eventually, embroidery, too. It didn't take long before I started combining my new hobbies with my lifelong passion for fashion.

"Why didn't you say anything about your art?" Nora asked.

Tears threatened as I realized it had been a long time since somebody described my designs as "art." I shook my head, hoping that was all it would take to make the tears (and this conversation) go away. "I . . . I haven't made anything in a long time."

"Do you think you might ever . . . " she trailed off.

"Do I think I might ever design again?" I shrugged. "Maybe. Probably not." Nora's hopeful smile fell from her face. *Great. Just another person for me to disappoint.* "Just put them back where you found them, okay?"

"Fine." She reluctantly tucked the portfolio back inside the drawer.

Maybe I should have asked her to toss them out altogether. It had been years since I'd even thought about sketching. And yet, something compelled me to hang onto them. As a memory for what was, a token for what could have been, or a vision for what still could be, who knew?

Maybe I was a masochist.

No, that's not it. There's a reason you've never gotten a tattoo.

We continued packing in silence, our off-off-off Broadway performance forgotten. By the time four o'clock rolled around and we'd finished loading up Devin's Mazda, the living room and bedroom were nearly box-free. All that remained were a few more knick-knacks that still needed to be packed, plus some larger furniture that we'd bring over tomorrow in the U-Haul Bowie had insisted on paying for.

"Just so you know," Nora said, slamming the trunk down and wrapping her arm around my shoulder. "If you ever do decide to make *that* dress, you better make it for me."

I tugged on the hand around my shoulder, pulling her closer. "You got it.

"I'm serious. I'd wear the *shit* out of it."

"I'd expect nothing less."

Killian

"Bring it in," I shouted, the blare of the whistle still echoing through my ears.

I shifted from side to side, trying to alleviate some of the pressure on my injured knee. This was the first week of training and I'd be lying if I said my body wasn't feeling it, even from the sidelines. It'd been a while since I'd spent so long on my feet.

"You alright, coach?" my assistant coach, Zia, asked.

"Just a bit stiff." She nodded. Like me, Zia was a retired footballer. She knew the aches and pains—emotional and physical—that came with a career like ours, some of which never went away. Unlike me, she had chosen to leave her professional football career. I envied her for that—a group of teens texting on their phones while driving had taken that choice from me. Then again, I couldn't imagine a better post-retirement setup than coaching with another athlete I respected, and who respected the game. I'd like to think she'd say the same about me. Plus, ever since she'd met her girlfriend, Blair, on the flight from London to Los Angeles no less, she now had *two* reasons to stay in California.

"Alright, team," I said, addressing the half-circle of players in front of me. They might call it women's soccer, but I'd never address this group as *ladies*. They were fierce, skilled athletes, and they deserved to be addressed as such. "By the time the holidays are out, we'll have less than three months to go Judging by the way some of you are huffing and puffing, it might take that long to get back to peak physical condition. Did *anybody* use the weight room during your break? No, wait, please don't tell me."

A few of them laughed. A few groaned. A few were still bent over, holding their sides thanks to the conditioning drill we'd just wrapped up.

"In all seriousness, I'm very pleased with everybody's progress this week. And uh," I paused, nudging the pitch with my toes. It needed to be said, but I wanted to make sure it was said the right way. "I think we've all been given an incredible opportunity to be here. A second or third chance even. And I count myself in there as well."

The South Bay Sounders might be the newest team in the National Women's Soccer League, but most of the players were well-seasoned, to say the least. Several were past their so-called "prime," while a few others had had some issues "gelling" with their previous teams. Whatever the reason, I'd helped handpick every athlete on this squad, along with the coaching staff. It was the *only* condition I'd requested in my contract, and thankfully, the team owner had agreed.

"So, let's make the most of it. Alright, that's enough from me. We're here Monday, nine a.m. sharp." They all nodded. "Great work. Hit the showers."

I'd already turned to go when Cheyenne, the co-captain from New Orleans, stopped me. "Coach, do you mind if I make an announcement about the holiday party?"

This time, I was the one groaning. "Right, get on with it."

Cheyenne had decided that a team holiday party would be the perfect opportunity for everyone to get to know each other and their families.

The team directed their attention her way. "Okay! Team holiday shindig is officially December 23rd, eight p.m. at Sparrow in Santa Monica. The banquet hall is ours until midnight. Bring your husbands, your wives, your Tinder date for the evening, *Emily.*"

"Ay-o!" somebody shouted. Probably Emily, Cheyenne's co-captain. A cackle of cheers went up from the rest of them.

"Please also bring a wrapped toy for the toy drive, and most importantly, *please,*" she said, adding several "e's" to the word, "leave your kids at home."

This time, their cheers echoed through the empty stadium.

"That's it!"

"Coach," Emily said, singling me out. "You're coming, right?"

My chest tightened. I rubbed a hand across the back of my neck and answered, "Oh, I don't know."

"You have to come!"

"My girlfriend wants to meet you."

"My husband is a huge fan of yours!"

Their cries rang out, one after another. I could feel Zia's lingering stare on the back of my neck, which I'd almost rubbed raw. I could do pep talks. I could manage post-game interviews, so long as I had some notes and a pen to click in my pocket. What I could not and did not do was make small talk amongst a roomful of strangers.

"We'll see," I told them, blowing out a strangled breath.

"But coach . . ."

"Great practice, everybody. Goodnight!"

I practically jogged off the field, injury be damned.

I wasn't sure what I was expecting when I walked into my house later that night, bag of takeout from my favorite Thai restaurant in hand, but it certainly wasn't this. Moving boxes were everywhere. A turquoise desk that had seen better days was smack dab in the middle of the entry way. Clothing was strewn about the living room. My eyes caught on a pair of fire-engine red knickers. Lace.

Fuck, is she trying to kill me?

"Nora?" the murderer in question called down the stairs. "Would you please grab the floral bag on your way back up? By the way, the shower curtain is cute, but it's a pain in the ass to hang up."

I set the food down on the counter and scoured the room for the bag. It didn't take me long to find the floral print amongst a sea of cardboard. Crab Rangoon would have to wait a few minutes.

I carried the bag up the floating staircase, a feature I still wasn't completely sold on but, according to my property agent, was to be expected in most modern houses these days. Not that I'd been looking specifically for a modern *house*. I'd spent the bulk of my footy career living out of high-rise condos and five-star hotels. Alone.

Don't be daft, you know you prefer it that way.

That was true. My anxiety had proven to be "too much" for some past partners and I didn't (typically) gravitate toward the idea of living with a stranger. So, I'd become very accustomed to living on my own.

What I'd also become accustomed to in recent years were "luxury finishes"—stainless steel appliances, marble countertops, a deep-soaker tub for those days when my knee acted up—all of which were readily available in West L.A. properties. It wasn't that I needed them. If anything, they were a nice reminder of where I'd come from and what I'd accomplished.

"Nora?" Leighton's voice floated down the hall, like a siren luring a sailor to sweet, unsuspecting doom. I found her in the guest bathroom, straddling the toilet lid, struggling to secure the final few hooks of a shower curtain with . . .

Are those bare bottoms?

I made a mental note to eventually ask why she'd traded the perfectly fine, grey shower curtain that had been hanging there this morning for the new one covered in illustrated, nude asses. For the time being, I was having a hard time focusing on anything other than the expanse of bare skin peeking out just above Leighton's ass. *God bless the person who invented crop tops. And leggings.* What would she do if I tickled that stripe of exposed skin, I wondered. Better yet, licked it?

Snap out of it, you sod.

"I should probably tell you that this shower isn't working."

Her balance wavered and I leapt forward. For a split second, I worried that she and the curtain might come tumbling down altogether. And wouldn't that be the perfect start to her stay? Thankfully, she righted herself, clicking the final curtain hook into place before hopping down from the toilet.

"Excuse me?" she said, her voice challenging, determined. This was a woman ready to wage war. I'd count myself lucky to be one of her casualties.

"Sorry to disappoint you, love. It's out of order until I can get a new showerhead." I tried (and failed) not to smile when I added, "You'll just have to share mine."

I tell you, if looks could fucking kill.

I couldn't be sure how long we stood there like that, face to, well, shoulder blades, one breath away from warfare. This was a game I was very familiar with. Sizing up the opponent, the enemy. Then again, I didn't think I'd ever been faced with such an intimidating creature in all my years on the pitch.

At some point, she noticed the bag in my hands. "Where's Nora?"

"I passed her on my way in, taking a call." It didn't escape me that she'd changed the subject, but I'd play along. I took a small step forward until her floral bag was the only thing separating the two of us. "Anything I can help with?"

Her demeanor changed completely. One second, she was eyeing me with an accusatory look on her face, and the next, she was smiling. Not a sweet, appreciative smile one might expect when offered help. No, this was a calculated, *"I know something you don't know,"* kind of smile.

Lord, I wanted to know all of Leighton Wheatley's smiles.

"Sure," she said sweetly. *Too* sweetly. "Why don't you go ahead and unpack that bag in this drawer?" She gestured toward the empty middle drawer of the floating vanity. Another *floating* feature in this house.

I turned my attention to the bag, easing the zipper open one inch at a time. Judging by the wicked grin on Leighton's face, I half expected a feral animal to claw me at any second. Thankfully, there were no animals to be found within, no deadly weapons of any kind. Just some boxes of . . .

You've got to be kidding me.

The tension in my shoulders eased. Did she honestly think *this*, of all things, would scare me? Intimidate me?

"Do you have a preference for how they're organized?"

Her smile fell, replaced by a look of befuddlement. Clearly, not the response she'd been anticipating. "What?"

"If there's a way you'd like them organized, please let me know." I thrust my hand into the bag, drawing out a handful of plastic tubes. "Tampons on one side, pads on the other? Do you separate out the liners? Different sizes for different flows?"

She shook her head, bewildered. "Why is it that you know so much about feminine hygiene products?"

"Did you think I'd be embarrassed, Leia? I know how women's bodies work. I'm a thirty-two-year-old man, not some teenage boy who doesn't know the mechanics of a woman's pussy."

I took pleasure in the comical way her jaw dropped, like something out of a Bugs Bunny cartoon. Not that Bugs Bunny ever went around discussing tampons and pussies.

Or maybe I missed that episode?

Without waiting for further instruction, I began filling the drawer as I saw fit. Pads on one side, tampons on the other. She could always go back and change it later. It only took a couple of minutes. When I stood back up to full height, I couldn't help but smirk. In the year I'd known Leighton, I'd never known her to be speechless. This was a woman who always had the last word in every conversation. Until today.

"Let me know if you need help moving anything else." I turned back toward the door but stopped for one final parting shot. "By the way, dinner's getting cold. I didn't know what you liked, so I got one of everything."

Chapter Three

December 7th

Leighton

A *m I dead or dreaming?*

It was a question I'd pondered daily since "moving in" with Killian. The better question was whether he was trying to kill me or if I was just *that* horny?

For the third day in a row, I'd woken up drenched in sweat and um, other fluids, after yet *another* restless night of X-rated dreams starring me and my annoyingly sexy roommate. Killian eating me out on the kitchen counter. Killian bending me over the kitchen island and fucking me from behind. Killian gripping my hips, rough enough to leave marks, while I rode his pierced dick in the pool out back. Because in my dreams, his dick was pierced.

Not that I had any interest in pool sex because hello, STIs. I'd also seen the movie *Showgirls* at a very formative age, and it was safe to say that I still hadn't recovered from the infamous pool scene.

But that didn't mean I couldn't think about it. And boy, had I thought about it. Vividly. It also hadn't helped that for the last three mornings, after I'd put my favorite vibrator to good use—*note to self, add batteries to my shopping list*—I'd come down the stairs to find the star of my fantasies swimming laps in the pool.

Naked.

Not that I could see much. The man glided through water like a fucking mermaid, kicking up waves in his wake. Good form, but bad luck for anybody trying to . . . sneak a peek.

That hadn't stopped me from trying.

Here I was, still wiping the sleep (or lack thereof) from my eyes, watching the water sluice over every tight, tattooed inch of Killian's body. That was another thing. I knew he had tattoos—we'd gone camping with Nora and Bo earlier this year and he'd spent most of the trip shirtless—but I hadn't realized just how much of his body was covered in ink. But it seemed like every stroke, every kick, every flip—*oh god, the flips*—revealed yet another lick of ink.

I'd lick that ink. All the way down to his . . .

The phone I'd tucked into my pajama pants pocket buzzed against my thigh, sending delicious shivers up my spine. Thankful for the timely interruption, I pulled it out to see a text message from my sister.

(Nelly) *FaceTime?*

(Me) *Not before I've had my coffee.*

As soon as I learned how to use the dang thing. Everything in Killian's house was what I considered "fancy pants," from the top-of-the-line bathroom fixtures to the marble fireplace and, of course, his Finnish coffee maker. It'd been three days and I still hadn't figured out how to turn the *Flur-der-bur* fucker on.

(Nelly) *When can I get a tour of the McMansion?*

She didn't wait for me to respond.

(Nelly) *And the McMillionaire?!*

I looked up from my spot by the stairs just as his royal fancy pants lifted himself over the edge of the pool. If there had been any doubt in mind that he swam naked, there wasn't anymore.

The McMillionaire had McBuns of steel.

I watched as he (tragically) wrapped a towel around his waist, tucking himself away before I could confirm my pierced dick theory. I knew that any second now, he'd turn around and catch me spying on him. It'd be impossible to miss, what with an entire wall of floor-to-ceiling windows. And yet, I couldn't be bothered to look away. Not when he was shaking the water out of his dirty-blond locks like a goddamn centerfold spread.

Well, at least I have something new to dream about tonight.

I wiped the drool from the corner of my mouth and texted my sister back.

(Me) *I'll call you later.*

"Good morning."

The familiar British lilt jolted me back to reality. I turned to face him. The way he was leaning against the sliding glass door did wonders for his biceps. And my fluttering vagina.

Enough. "It'd be better if I could figure out how to use your robo-coffee pot."

A dopey smile spread across his face, adding to my aggravation. He tucked his hair behind his ears. "I'll show you."

We met at the coffee pot. "First thing you want to do is—"

"Hold on a second," I said, gently elbowing my way around him. "I can't see through you, Thor."

"My mistake." He held up his hands, allowing me to scoot closer until the coffee pot was directly in front of me.

"Okay, ready."

It only took a second for me to recognize my error in judgment. But it was long enough for Killian to wrap his behemoth arms around me and rest one on either side of the coffee pot. *Crap.*

"Alright, so first thing you want to do . . ."

I tried to listen as he very matter-of-factly explained the step-by-step process. I really did. But my listening skills were no defense against the damp towel pressing against my backside. It didn't escape me that the space between us was getting smaller by the second. Every lift of a lever that did who knew what, every press of a button that turned something (not me, definitely not me) on, it all brought his body closer to mine. I suddenly regretted the fact that I hadn't put on a bra or underwear before coming downstairs. There wasn't much separating his potentially pierced cock from the heat of my pussy. Just a towel that probably cost more than I made in a month and some threadbare boxers I'd bought in a value pack from Target.

It would be so easy to . . .

"Got it?"

"What?" I asked, looking up and over my shoulder. I'd never been with anybody who made me feel so petite. Not that we were together, but still.

"Need me to go over it again?"

"I'm good," I squeaked, all thoughts of caffeine cleared from my mind. What I needed was another romp with my vibrator.

"Right." He paused. "Do you mind if I use the shower first?" he asked, his warm breath tickling my ear. Was I imagining things or had his voice dropped an octave? I could feel my pulse racing, matched only by the *bum-bum-bum* zipping through my pussy. It took a special kind of person to make your heart *and* pussy beat so hard.

Apparently, Killian was special.

"All yours."

I could've sworn I heard him whisper under his breath, something like, *"Do you mean it?"* I didn't ask.

Instead, I waited until I felt him pull away, until I heard his footsteps clear the stairs, before turning around to catch my breath. Who knew that making coffee, a typically mundane and nonsexual task, would turn out to be such an erotic experience?

Rather than dwell too deeply on the fact that three days in Killian's house had proved more sexually stimulating than my last three relationships combined, I video-called my sister.

"That was fast!" Janelle remarked, her smile lighting up the other side of the screen. Even though it was Sunday morning, she was already showered and dressed, not a hair or freckle out of place. I had no doubt she'd already been to the gym, answered emails, and probably cured world hunger, too. All before noon.

"Are you okay?" she asked. "Your face is all flushed."

"I'm fine," I grumbled. "I woke up on the wrong side of the Mc-Mansion." My eyes caught on a familiar NSYNC poster behind her. "Are you at Mom and Dad's?"

"How could you tell?" She turned the phone toward our childhood bedroom. I hoped that someday, historians would study this well-preserved site as a snapshot of 90s teen culture. If the NSYNC and Jonathan Taylor Thomas posters didn't give it away, the inflatable purple chair and inactive subscription to *Cosmo Girl* magazine on the nightstand would. "Winter came early in Ohio. The internet's out in my building, so I'm stuck here until it's back up."

"I almost didn't recognize what Mom's done with the place," I said, sarcasm dripping from my lips.

"I'm pretty sure she hasn't had the carpet cleaned since the great nail polish disaster of 2003, either. It still reeks of acetone."

She settled into the mountain of tiny pillows on her bed. "But enough small talk. I want to see the McMansion!"

I sighed. "Nell, there are still boxes everywhere."

"Please, Leigh. I'm stressing over the fact that it's already December and I haven't heard back about my exam. I'm sleeping in my childhood bedroom. I need the distraction."

"Are Mom and Dad home?"

"They're still at Cakes with Claus."

I rolled my eyes. Our mother had chaired the committee for Cakes with Claus, an annual pancake breakfast fundraiser where locals could eat pancakes with Santa, for as long as I could remember. The knowledge that there were a decade's worth of photos of Nellie and I dressed like elves circulating the internet somewhere haunted me to this very day.

"Fine." I huffed.

For the next ten minutes, I took her through every room of the house, excluding Killian's bedroom and en suite, where the shower was still running. By the time we finished, I'd planted myself in the farthest end of the couch, closest to the roaring fire, and Nellie was still scraping her jaw off the floor.

"Are you sure you don't want to marry this guy?"

I rolled my eyes. "Yeah, because that wouldn't be messy."

"Every relationship is messy."

"No, thank you. I'm already trying to clean up my last mess."

She frowned. "You're too hard on yourself, Leigh."

I picked at the nonexistent lint on my shorts. Anything to distract me from this conversation. "I know, but—"

"Janelle, we brought you a to-go box. You better come eat before it gets cold."

Oh no.

"I'm on the phone, Mom," Nellie called over her shoulder, through the closed door. Not that it would make much of a difference. There wasn't a door, lock, or vault that could keep Wanda Wheatley out if she wanted in. The woman wanted to know everything about everyone every moment of the day. And if somebody was on the phone in *her* house, it was only a matter of time before . . .

The door burst open.

"Is that our Leia?" Mom asked, snatching the phone from Nellie's hands.

I sighed audibly. There was a reason I loathed Killian's nickname for me. I'd heard it for the first thirty years of my life ad nauseam.

"Hi, Mom," I said, forcing a smile. "It's great to see you, but we were about to hang up. I've got to get to work."

"Hank! Get in here," she yelled over her shoulder, making both Nellie and I wince. On a scale of one to ten, Wanda Wheatley's default volume was eleven.

As if summoned by a magical entity—and honestly, learning that our mother was a witch wouldn't surprise me in the least—my dad appeared, mustache first, belly second. I gritted my teeth.

"Hi, Dad."

"Hey, kiddo. Do you remember Lottie Murtaugh's niece?"

I racked my brain. "Um, I'm not sure."

"Brown hair. I think you went to junior high with her." *Oh, right. Her.* "You don't remember her?" he asked with genuine shock.

"Do you have anything else for me to go on?" I asked, doing my best to suppress every eye-rolling, sarcastic urge in my body. "Like maybe her name?"

"I don't know." He shrugged. "Starts with a D, or maybe an L. I can't believe you don't remember her."

Kill me. Kill me now.

"Sorry, that's not ringing any bells. Was there something about Lottie Murtaugh's niece you wanted to tell me?"

"She's pregnant."

"With her *third* baby," my mom added.

"Wow. Great."

"You don't sound very excited," my dad admonished. I could feel my temperature rising.

"How excited would you like me to be about an unnamed girl with brown hair that I *may* have gone to school with twenty years ago having another baby?"

"You don't have to be such a smart ass about it, kiddo. All I'm saying—"

"Shower's free, Leia," I heard from behind me. As it turned out, there was something imperfect about Killian: his timing.

"Who's that, kiddo?" Dad asked just before Mom pointed beyond me and shouted, "Hanky, that's not her apartment. Leia, whose house are you in?"

And just as I felt the bile begin to rise in my throat, just as the sound of Killian's bare feet descending the stairs rang through the room, my sister blurted out three words that changed the course of my Christmas. *Of my life.*

"That's her fiancé."

Killian

"That's her fiancé."

The room blurred as Leighton's sister's words echoed through my head. A drop of moisture—sweat or dew from the shower, I couldn't be sure— rolled down my back, burying itself beneath the band of my sweatpants. I was suddenly grateful I had forgone my post-swim protein shake because judging by the gurgling of my stomach, there'd be no keeping anything down right now.

As I broached the bottom of the stairs, everything slowly came back into focus, starting with the moving boxes still crowding the room and ending on the three sets of eyes staring back at me from Leighton's phone.

"That's her fiancé."

My palms were sweating harder than a pot of onions. I rubbed them on my sweats. I couldn't have picked a worse pair of trousers for meeting my future in-laws.

"That's her fiancé."

Hang on a second.

Maybe I could work with this. Maybe this was the opportunity I had been waiting for. Maybe I was going to vomit.

I chose not to focus on the butterflies doing somersaults in my belly and instead tucked my hands into my pockets—hopefully, in that effortless "cool guy" way I'd only seen in the movies—and descended the remaining few stairs.

"You were right, Leia. We should've told them."

I heard a gasp from the other side of the phone, followed by a woman's voice I didn't recognize asking, "He calls her Leia?" *Must be her mum.*

At the same time, another voice belonging to whom I assumed was her father grumbled, "He's British?"

I, on the other hand, only had eyes for Leighton, who, judging by her slightly ajar lips and blank expression, was floundering. And then, in an uncharacteristically prattish move I was sure we'd have words about later, I leaned forward, placed an arm on either side of her until she was caged into the corner of the couch, and dropped a kiss on her forehead. I couldn't say it was how I envisioned our first kiss, but it didn't make it any less glorious. For me, at least.

I dropped into the space beside her and pulled her to my side. Her body radiated tension. So, I did what any good fiancé with severe anxiety would do. I swallowed the fear oozing out of me, flipped the switch for "Confident Killian," the public facade I'd spent years cultivating, and prepared to kiss some major parental *arse*.

"Mr. and Mrs. Wheatley, I'm so sorry to spring this on you like this. It's entirely my fault that you didn't know sooner. *Leia* here," I said, emphasizing the nickname I'd given her a year ago, "was dying to tell you the good news, but selfishly, I wanted us to wait until we saw you in person." Until now, I hadn't known why the name bothered her so much. No wonder she'd always seem put off by me. "I suppose the cat's out of the bag now, though. Your incredible daughter has agreed to spend the rest of her life with me."

From the corner of my eye, I saw her mouth twist. I wasn't sure what soured her mood more, the fact that I'd played into this incredibly awkward situation or the prospect of spending the rest of her life with me. Hopefully, it was the former, but it didn't matter now. Her family would never buy this farce if she didn't play along.

"Isn't that right, *Leia*?" I nudged.

"Uh-huh," she said in disbelief. That wasn't going to cut it. Not if we wanted this to look remotely believable. I dropped my arm to her waist and pulled her closer, until she was practically on my lap. "Yep! That's right!" she squealed.

"Please forgive us for springing this on you, especially before you've had a chance to get to know me, but . . ." I turned toward my blushing bride-to-be. Blushing was putting it mildly. Leighton's face was approaching a dangerous shade of red, tinged with equal parts fury and embarrassment. I waited until her eyes met mine before adding, "I just couldn't imagine spending another day without her by my side."

I wasn't lying. But she didn't know that.

"Leia, why didn't you say anything?" her mom asked, sniffling. Lord, were they buying this?

"I, um . . ." Leighton's eyes searched mine. I couldn't tell if she found the answer she was looking for, because seconds later, she turned back to the phone still in her hand. "I didn't know how you'd react?"

I tore my gaze away from her and took a moment to study her family more closely. As close as one could through a four-inch phone screen. I was immediately taken aback by how young her parents looked. They couldn't be much older than fifty by my estimate, a stark contrast to Bowie's mums who were well into their late sixties.

My eyes flickered to the younger woman standing behind them who looked *nothing* like Leighton. Whereas Leighton was short and stacked, her sister, Janelle, was tall and lean. Leighton had thick, brown hair that barely touched her shoulders. Her sister's bouncy, blonde curls fell halfway down her back. In fact, the only piece of Leighton I recognized in her sister was the mischievous gleam in her eyes. Other than that, she didn't hold a candle to Leighton, as far as I was concerned.

Leighton was the candle, the flame, and the whole fucking matchbook.

"Well, we're a little bit surprised, kiddo," her dad mumbled, a slight Midwestern twang to his voice. "But other than that—"

"We're thrilled!" her mom shouted before jumping up and down like a toddler on Christmas morning. The phone in her hand bounced with her.

"Really?" Leighton asked, her voice tinged with worry.

"Of course! How could we not be?" Her mother settled into her father's side, much in the same way I was holding Leighton to mine. "Honey, you know we love how 'independent' you are. And how much you don't 'need' a husband."

"Or wife," her dad added, lifting a finger as if he'd just made some revolutionary statement. *By George, he's done it. He's discovered pansexuality.*

"That's right." Her mom smiled. "Because we're 'allies.'"

"Mom, why are you using air quotes?" Janelle asked.

"But your father and I were worried you would *never* find somebody. Like, *never.*"

"Mom, I'm thirty. Not eighty."

"Well, you're not getting any younger, baby. And speaking of *babies,* I'd prefer you to have some before *I'm* eighty."

Leighton froze, shell-shocked. Without thinking, I gently rubbed my thumb over her arm.

"Mom, I'm not . . . I mean, *we're not—*"

"Oh, there's plenty of time to talk babies, but first, we have a wedding to plan. Now, I know it's last minute, but if you want to reserve the church before next summer, I might be able to call in a favor from Maggie's cousin's botanist. The one who's married to Pastor Jim."

While her mom steamrolled, Leighton sunk farther into the couch, deep enough to the point where my arm was the only thing holding her up. I had noticed that like me, Leighton had a knack for trying to disappear, especially when the conversation turned personal or the room got too crowded. Until today, I'd always wondered what (or who) had caused her to feel that way. I now had my answer.

"Mrs. Wheatley, if I may?"

"Oh, please call me Mom."

"Er, alright, well, maybe we should table wedding talk until after the holidays." The last thing I needed was to make my fake future mother-in-law cross, so I added, "If that's alright with you, of course?"

Everyone waited. For what, I wasn't sure. Approval, maybe? It was clear that the Wheatley family lived and died by the word of its matriarch. I wasn't sure how much time passed before she spoke again. Long enough for me to count the creases of the fingers in my pocket. Twice.

"You're right," she finally answered. "We should focus on the holidays." Everybody released a collective sigh, me included. "I've got a wonderful idea! We'll spend the holidays with *you.*"

Well, bollocks.

"What? No. Mom," Leighton protested, scrambling to her feet. Unwilling to let go of her, I stood up, too. "You don't have to do that."

"Oh, but we want to. Right, Hank?"

"I don't know. We have that pickleball tournament on the twenty-seventh." Mrs. Wheatley's withering stare halted any further thought or mention of pickleball. "On second thought, we could do with some sunshine."

"Mom, it's already December. You don't have anything booked. It'll be next to impossible to find a place to stay this close to Christmas."

"Nonsense. Christmas is weeks away. Aunt Peg works for United, I'm sure she could spare us some miles." Apparently, Mrs. Wheatley carried around a Mary Poppins bag, full of practically perfect solutions for every problem. "And we'll stay with you, of course."

"Sorry?" I asked. At least, I thought it was me. The only other time I'd heard my voice reach such a high decibel was after I'd taken a ball to the groin during the 2012 semifinals. We'd lost the game and I'd spent the entire flight home with a bag of frozen peas strapped to my crotch.

"We won't take up much space," she said, waving a hand. "Would you rather we spend Christmas morning in a cold hotel room? You're future in-laws?"

I'd once read an article that said it takes ten thousand hours to *master* an artform. Judging by her exaggerated, wounded puppy eyes and quivering lip, I reckoned Mrs. Wheatley could teach the damn class on guilt-tripping.

An elbow to the side brought me back to the present. Leighton's family was waiting for an answer, and they weren't the only ones. I looked down into Leighton's eyes, begging, pleading for me to say no. I couldn't bear to disappoint or embarrass her, more so than I already had at least. That left one other option . . .

Scenario A: Tell the Wheatleys the truth. I feared that might place Leighton in a poorer light, even if the whole act was my idea.

Scenario B: Tell the Wheatleys to shove off and ruin any chance of winning their approval in the eventuality I one day married their daughter. Then again, it might put me in Leighton's good graces.

Scenario C: Run. Even with my bad knee, I could still pull a seven-minute mile.

Or Scenario D: The lesser of all evils, as far as I could tell.

Here goes nothing . . .

"We'd love to have you stay with us for Christmas, Mr. and Mrs. Wheatley." When I caught a glimpse of a blonde in the background, I added, "And your daughter, as well."

Leighton's mouth opened and closed wordlessly. But there was no need to say anything. I'd already sealed our fate and her mother more than made up for her daughter's silence.

"Delightful. We'll take care of the arrangements and let you know when we're flying in. Oh, this is going to be so much fun! Our first Christmas in Hollywood."

"Well, I live in Venice Beach—"

"We'll need to do some shopping once we get there, get the stuff for the games and pajamas. Oh, Leia! Be sure to send me your new address so I can mail the Christmas mice!"

Leighton winced.

"Mom, I don't know—"

"We can't wait to see you. Love you, bye!"

A cacophony of well-wishes and virtual smooches ended with the sudden click of a button. And then, nothing. Just the hiss of the coffee pot, the sound of the pool filter bobbing through the shallow water, and the bombardment of thoughts racing across my brain.

"What. Did. You. Just. Do." It wasn't a question, so much as an accusation. I turned to her, her eyes full of ire, arms-crossed over her chest, which only amplified the generous cleavage already peeking out of her pajama top. I pretended not to notice that she wasn't wearing a bra.

Reason #28: Boobs.

"Look, I know I probably shouldn't have said anything."

"You think?" she fired back.

"But your sister said I was your fiancé and I thought if I played along, maybe it would help—

"Well, it didn't. And now I'm fucked."

If only.

Almost as if she could read my mind, her face flushed. I briefly wondered what other parts of her body flushed when she was embarrassed, but now wasn't the time.

"Look," I said, softening my tone. "I know this isn't something either of us planned, but I'm happy to play the doting fiancé for a few weeks if that's what it takes to make your life a little bit easier."

She scoffed. "Believe me, there is nothing easy about my family."

"I kind of gathered that, but it's Christmas. Wouldn't it be nice to spend the holidays with your family? From the sound of things, you don't exactly have the . . . smoothest relationship with them."

"And you do with yours?" she asked defensively.

I smiled sadly. "My family's dead."

If possible, her cheeks heated further. I held up a hand when she opened her mouth. "And before you go apologizing for something you had nothing to do with, please don't. It was an observation, not a judgment. I would never judge you, princess."

"Princess?" she asked, confusion washing over her face.

"Well, you *clearly* don't like Leia. I feel like a prick, by the way. I wish you had told me."

"It's okay."

"*So,* princess it is. Unless you prefer general?"

She smiled. An irresistible, captivating smile that, in turn, made me grin like a fool.

"Why are you doing this for me?" she asked. "You've already given me a place to stay, one I can by no means afford, and yet here I am. Now you want to be my pretend boyfriend—"

"Fiancé," I corrected. At least one of us needed to take our very fake relationship status seriously.

"What do you get out of any of this?"

You. I didn't tell her how being her fiancé, regardless of how long it lasted, would be an honor, not a burden. I didn't tell her how much it pained me to see her so suspicious of somebody, a friend, offering to help. I didn't tell her any of what I wanted to say, what I needed to say.

Instead, I offered, "A date to my team's Christmas party?"

Her eyebrows drew together and her jaw tightened. I knew she was weighing her options, perhaps running a few scenarios of her own. Any second, I was expecting her to rush up the stairs and re-pack her bags. Any second, she'd call a Lyft and hightail it out of here. Any second—

"Deal." She thrust her hand out toward me.

Reason #42: She never fails to surprise me.

"Deal." I tried to contain my smile when I took her hand in mine, thankful that my sweat had subsided. What surprised me more was the fact that she didn't immediately retreat, not until my thumb ghosted across her knuckles. Only then did she pull her hand away and tuck it awkwardly to her side.

"I guess I'll shower now."

I nodded, watching as she walked toward the stairs. I'd spent the last three nights jacking off to the thought of her soaping her body in *my* shower.

Better to save those thoughts for later, when you're not wearing trackies.

When she was halfway up the stairs, I called up to her. "Also, I prefer killjoy."

"What?" She scrunched her eyebrows together, confused.

"Before, you called me Thor. But I like it better when you call me killjoy."

"You do know that's supposed to be an insult, right?" she explained slowly, as if I were a child. "I was teasing you."

"Yes, but only *you* call me killjoy," I said, grinning smugly. "And I like it when my *fiancée* teases me."

The intense shade of pink blossoming on her cheeks told me everything I needed to know. My *fiancée* liked it when I teased her, too. And suddenly, Christmas wasn't looking so bad after all.

Chapter Four

December 12th

Leighton

Five days.

That was how long it took my family to plan, book, and board their flight to LAX. During one of the busiest travel times of the year, no less. Which meant I'd had five days to not only unpack every moving box, but also to decorate Killian's 3,000-square-foot home, a daunting task to say the least.

"Alright, that should do it," he said, placing the last bottle brush Christmas tree on the mantel. He stepped back to admire our work, and yes, it was *our* work. Between the unpacking and the decorating, Killian had helped every step of the way. When I'd let him, of course.

I'd told him in no uncertain terms that my mom would give me endless crap if she didn't arrive to *some* holiday décor. Like a true modern gentleman, he'd given me carte blanche with his Visa at Home-Goods. I'd reluctantly spent his money on pom-pom garland, bright and colorful throw pillows—because silver and gold would never do for Wanda Wheatley—and stockings for us all, which Killian had promptly "hung by the fire with care."

"Well, now, isn't this lovely?"

I nodded. "Yep, it's a good start."

I only wish I'd had a camera to capture his look of astonishment.

"*Start?* I'd say it's plenty, don't you think?"

Amateur. We might have made a small dent in covering up the neutral whites and grays throughout the main living space, but Killian had no idea who he was dealing with.

"Oh, *darling,*" I drew out sarcastically."As you will learn soon enough, there is never enough Christmas as far as my family is concerned. Fun fact for you, my mother is an award-winning table-setter."

Speaking of the table . . .

I carefully unwrapped the red-and-white striped candlesticks and began to dress the dining table. A glance at the Santa clock in the kitchen told me they'd be arriving any minute. We'd offered to pick them up at the airport, but my dad had insisted they rent their own car. My parents didn't travel much and if I had to guess, I'd say he had plans to use this as his one and (maybe) only opportunity to drive some flashy luxury car.

It would indeed be a Christmas miracle if my mother allowed that.

"Beg your pardon?"

"Oh, yes. Wanda Wheatley is a thrice-decorated blue ribbon champion at the Franklin County Fair. Best Winter Tablescape, Best Budget-Friendly Tablescape, and Most Original Use of Tinsel."

His head whirled like a bobblehead, and yet the messy bun atop his head never wavered. "That cannot be a real thing."

"Her awards are framed and hanging next to our baby photos." He blew out a strained breath. "Well, it's going to have to do for now. Did we get everything?"

"Far as I can tell." He rubbed a hand over his freshly trimmed beard. "Oh, I did get something else." He hesitated briefly before trotting off toward the garage.

"Not a tree, I hope," I called out just as the door closed behind him. "Or a ring!" I'd been very clear that choosing the Christmas tree together was a Wheatley family tradition, something we should wait on until my family's arrival. The ring was a hard limit for me as well, despite Killian's protests. As I explained to him, we wanted to "sell" my family on our engagement, but at the end of the day, our relationship wasn't real. There would be no wedding. There would be no honeymoon. And there was no way I was willing to accept a real rock from my fake fiancé.

Maybe for my next fake engagement.

A few minutes passed with no sign of Killian and whatever he'd gone to fetch. I had just decided to follow him when he returned, his arms full of . . . picture frames?

"I, uh . . ." *Is he blushing?* It was hard to tell what was happening beneath that beard. "I thought it might look more believable if we had some photos. Of us."

"Us? You and me, us?"

He laid his bounty across the couch cushions. There we were. At the tearoom, camping with Nora and Bowie, trick-or-treating with the kids Nora used to nanny for. I'd worn my favorite oversized, lavender hoodie and a pair of aviators, my go-to, lazy-girl cosplay of Damian from *Mean Girls*. Killian looked like he'd come straight from work. As he told it, he'd dressed as Coach Beard from *Ted Lasso*.

There was even one of just the two of us outside Bowie's house. I couldn't tell you what we'd been talking about or even when the photo had been taken, but from the outside perspective, it looked like a happy couple. A private moment captured on film.

Amazing still was the fact that I'd fought tooth and nail to avoid this man as much as possible for nearly a year and yet, here he was, beside me in nearly a dozen photos. Here he was, beside me now, prepared to face down my family.

"Wow."

"Do you like them?" I must've hesitated a beat too long because he quickly added, "It's okay if you don't. I can fill the empty space with some art or something. We can go back to HomeGoods."

"I love them."

"Oh," he said, though it was more of an exhalation of breath.

"That was a . . . good idea. Thank you," I all but forced out. He smiled then.

"You don't have to sound so put out about it."

I bit my lip to hide a smile of my own then went back to perusing the photos. Amongst the many of us and our friends were a few from years past. One of him in his soccer uniform, surrounded by teammates. Another with him and Bowie when they were teenagers, maybe. One photo in particular, the smallest of the bunch, caught my eye.

"Is that you?"

"Yes."

"And your mom?"

"Yes."

"How old are you there?"

"Twelve, to the day." He sounded so certain. "It was taken on my birthday. If you look closely, you can see the Kool-Aid stain on my jumper."

My smile widened. In between work and decorating, we'd spent the last few days learning more about each other. Our families, our pasts, our allergies. No coconut for Killian. I'd walked him through the overwhelming amount of Wheatley winter holiday traditions he was about to be subjected to. He'd given me an up-close (but not as personal as I would've preferred) tour of his tattoos. I'd answered all his questions about growing up with a sister. Like Bowie, he was an only child, so different family dynamics fascinated him. He'd schooled me on U.K. slang, food, and geography, which led me to conclude that there was a lot more to miss about the U.K. than my sleepy hometown of Plain, Ohio. The name said it all. Our only claim to fame was *Cornhenge,* an art installation of over one hundred concrete ears of corn.

Because Ohio.

It wasn't all tattoos and nutcrackers, though. In between the happy memories and anecdotes, we also touched on some of the darker moments in our lives. Then again, my case of eldest daughter syndrome didn't seem nearly as bad once I heard about Killian's childhood.

"It was the last birthday I had with her."

Killian's mom, Justine, had unfortunately lost her battle with Ovarian cancer just before his next birthday. And since his father had never been part of the picture, he'd spent his teen years bouncing between foster homes and Bowie's couch. If offering me a rent-free place to live hadn't changed my mind about Killian, hearing him talk about his upbringing by a single mother in a low-income housing certainly had.

I couldn't believe I'd been so—to borrow a word from Killian's tutorial—daft. He wasn't some self-centered man-baby with a trust fund, but rather a generous, self-sufficient cinnamon roll with a penchant for bath bombs and *Murder, She Wrote.*

He was a goddamn unicorn.

As he continued studying the photo of him and his mom, I fought every instinct to reach out and touch him, hug him. I'd bet all of *Cornhenge* that this gentle giant gave incredible hugs, but the last thing either of us needed was to blur the lines. He was my best friend's best friend turned roommate turned fake fiancé. Nothing more, nothing less. Simple as that.

"We should put the photos up," I told him. "They'll be here any second."

"Right."

We spent the next ten minutes in silence, scattering photos across the walls, end tables, and even a couple on the mantel. Front and center. When my sister texted that they were a few miles out, we walked outside to greet them. I tried to suppress the shivers racking my body while we waited in Killian's well-paved, well-manicured yard. In my haste to meet my family, I'd stupidly forgotten a sweatshirt.

"Here," Killian said, his outstretched hand offering me his hoodie, the South Bay Sounders logo embroidered just above the front left pocket.

"Thank you." I was too cold to argue.

I tucked my arms through the sleeves, which ended well-past my fingertips, and tilted my nose toward the shoulder.

Mm, smells like . . . sweat and sandalwood.

"It's clean, I promise."

Great. He'd caught me sniffing his sweatshirt. "I believe you."

Just as I spotted a car turn onto the street, he spoke softly from over my shoulder. When had he moved closer to me?

"You know, there's probably one more thing you should know before we do this. Something that any person would know about their fiancé."

I angled my body toward him. "What's that?"

He gently tugged the sides of the hoodie until I had no choice but to step forward, closing the gap between us. I sucked in a breath, which only pressed my breasts farther into his well-sculpted chest.

"How I kiss."

Killian

In all the hours I'd spent fantasizing about my first *real* kiss with Leighton Wheatley, not once had I imagined it would happen in my driveway, next to the begonia bushes. On a Tuesday night. And yet, somehow, I'd known that kissing her would change my life.

That this would be my last first kiss.

Hers, too. Even if she didn't know it yet. Leighton was endgame, and now was the time to start laying the groundwork. Starting with kissing the shit out of her here and now, begonias and all.

My hands drifted from the hoodie I'd given her to the luscious curves of her hips, taking purchase there. Finally, I understood why people called them "love handles." I wanted to grip them and hang on tight—while she rode my face, while I plowed into her from be-hind—until my hands left a permanent mark.

I tightened my grip and swallowed her gasp of surprise, using my tongue to tease her lips open. It only took a second or so for her to respond, for her fervor to match my own. From there, it was a duel. A fight to the finish, only this fight didn't have any losers.

Her hands slid up my torso, past my shoulders until they tangled greedily in the hair escaping my bun. A jolt of pleasure-pain zipped through me as I imagined my head between her thighs, her hands coursing through my hair once again, only this time to coax my tongue deeper in her pussy.

Little did she know, there'd be no coaxing necessary. I'd count myself lucky to eat her for breakfast, lunch, and dinner, twice on Sundays.

The nearby slam of a car door pulled me out of my fantasy, but I wasn't about to end this kiss prematurely. Not even for her family. This tongue-fucking had been a year in the making.

Instead, I used my hands to ease her away, slowly separating our mouths millimeter by millimeter without letting go of her hips. When I opened my eyes, I couldn't help but smirk at the dazed, awestruck look on her face. She stared up at me with those beautiful brown eyes, unsteady breaths filtering through her full lips made fuller from my kisses. There was no hiding the length of my cock straining against the zipper of my trousers. I knew she could feel me. Hopefully, her parents wouldn't notice.

"Well, this is quite the welcome."

She jumped away from my hold like a teenager who had just been caught making out by her parents. In all fairness, she had been.

"Hi, Mom." She wrapped her arms around Mrs. Wheatley, a petite woman whose blonde hair was starting to grey. She hugged her father and sister as well before asking, "How was your flight?"

"Long," Janelle answered begrudgingly, eyes rolling back into her skull.

"It would've felt a lot shorter if your father wasn't snoring the entire way."

"I don't snore," Mr. Wheatley grumbled.

"Hank, who are you trying to fool?" Mrs. Wheatley shook her head. "But Peg got us upgraded to business class, so we got an extra bag of pretzels. Here, I saved one just for you, Killian." Mrs. Wheatley reached into her purse, drawing out a crinkly bag and thrusting it into my hand.

"Oh. Thank you." Because how else were you meant to respond when your FFMIL (fake future-mother-in-law) gave you a free airline snack?

"It might not be *Walkers Crisps*," she said, throwing me an exaggerated wink, "but still good."

"How do you know about Walkers?" I hadn't seen the U.K. favorite since I'd moved to the States. What I wouldn't give for a bag of my favorite snack, smoky bacon flavor preferred.

"I did my research."

"She made a Pinterest board," Janelle snarked. "Named it 'Merry Britmas.'"

"I'm about to have a British son-in-law. Naturally, I need to brush up on my U.K. knowledge." Her eyes lit up. "Wow! Hank, look at this place. I feel like we're staying at a resort."

"Mm-hmm," he said, pursing his lips. I was beginning to think that Hank's default setting was grinch.

"I like the car, Dad." Leighton nodded her head toward the Ford Focus parked beside my mailbox. "Very sensible."

"Don't remind me."

"Do you have some wine, Killian?" Wanda asked. "Maybe a Cabernet?" How anybody over the age of twenty-five could have this much energy after nine p.m. was beyond me. I could barely keep my eyes open, and Wanda Wheatley was ready for a Tuesday night rager.

"You had three on the plane," Hank whispered, not softly enough though.

"Sure," I told her. "Let's go in and get comfortable."

I opened the door for them, letting them all pass while keeping an eye on Leighton bringing up the rear. Her expression was indecipherable, a combination of fear, confusion, and anxiety maybe?

"Oh, this is lovely!" Mrs. Wheatley exclaimed when she crossed the threshold. "But honey, where are the rest of your Christmas decorations?"

Leighton flashed me a pained look. I smiled back at her.

It's going to be a long two weeks.

"Have you thought about marigold?"

"The flower?"

"No, the color. For bridesmaid dresses."

"Mom," Leighton said, the stress resonating in her voice. "Can we not do wedding talk right now?"

My head ping-ponged back and forth between Leighton and Mrs. Wheatley. Wanda. My mother might not be around anymore, but I couldn't imagine calling anybody else "Mum." Thankfully, Mrs. Wheatley understood, so after another bottle of wine (and two glasses of scotch for Mr. Wheatley), we settled on Wanda. Unfortunately, Mr. Wheatley was still Mr. Wheatley.

"There's just so much to think about. And where's your ring?"

Pink spread across Leighton's cheeks. "It's, um, in . . . ," she said, stumbling over her words.

"It's getting resized," I offered, taking her hand in mine and resting it on my thigh. "That's my fault, I'm afraid. I completely bungled the ring size." I rested my thumb on her pulse point, which was beating raggedly. I wasn't sure if that was because of our physical contact or the barrage of lies.

"Well, I'm whooped." Wanda climbed to her feet. "We've been up since six, so I think it's time to call it a night. C'mon, Hank."

We followed them upstairs, helping with the luggage. Wanda alone had three full-sized suitcases, though according to her, two of them were chock full of "Christmas essentials." Her words, not mine.

Things were off to a good start. I was just starting to believe that we might be able to pull this fiancé façade off for the next two weeks when Wanda and Mr. Don't-Call-Me-Hank Wheatley approached a door. Not just any door. No, this was the door that led to the guest room Leighton had slept in since she moved in. I knew then that we'd fucked up.

"No!" Leighton said, much too loudly. Loud enough for everyone to stop cold in the hall. "I meant, *that's* Nellie's room." She gestured toward the door in question. "Your room is at the end of the hall. It has a king-sized mattress and a walk-in closet for your stuff. *And* the perfect desk for present wrapping."

Apparently, that last factor sealed the deal. "Perfect! But first things first, tomorrow, we put up more decorations. *And* bake cookies for the neighbors." Wanda practically skipped down the hall to the guest room, Hank trailing dutifully behind her. I didn't bother mentioning that I didn't know the neighbors.

"Oh, Mom. The guest bathroom shower . . ."

"Has a brand-new nozzle," I interjected. "Just installed it today, so please let me know if the pressure's okay." Leighton's brow furrowed. She was probably wondering why I hadn't changed it sooner. I wondered how long it would take before she realized that I'd put it off strictly because I enjoyed the thought of her sharing *my* shower.

Wanda placed a hand to her heart. "Oh, he's handy, too? You better hang onto this one, Leia."

Her attention snapped back to her mother. "Er, yeah."

We waited until their door shut, leaving Leighton, Janelle, and I alone in the hallway. And that was when the whispering began.

"Let me sleep with you," Leighton demanded.

"No way," Janelle told her.

"All my stuff is in there."

"You should've thought of that before we got here. By the way, I love the framed photos. Excellent touch."

I didn't even get a chance to thank her before the heated exchange continued. Was this what it was like for all siblings?

"I need my stuff."

"Well, we'll move it into your room tomorrow."

"That is my room."

Janelle crossed her arms over her chest. "What did you think was going to happen when you invited us? As far as Mom and Dad are concerned, you're engaged. They might be old-fashioned, but they're not stupid. You really think they're going to buy you sleeping in a different room than your fiancé?"

"I. Did. Not. Invite. You." I could practically hear Leighton's teeth grinding. "This is all your fault. None of this would've happened if you wouldn't have lied to them."

"I was doing you a favor!" Janelle argued.

"Ladies, I hate to interrupt." That was a lie. Unless it was on the football pitch, fighting gave me hives, from the smallest argument to a heated confrontation. I could already feel the heat breaking out on my neck. "Janelle's right. It's going to look off if we're sleeping in separate rooms. That will only lead to questions, more questions than your mum already has."

Leighton chewed on my words, glancing back at her parents' closed door.

"She already scares the ever-loving the piss out of me. And your dad has barely said a word, which, frankly, is also frightening. I have no idea what the man is bloody thinking."

"Oh, he doesn't like you," Janelle said matter-of-factly.

"Sorry?"

Leighton shrugged. "Don't worry about it. He doesn't like anybody."

The three of us stood there silently, waiting for a decision to be made, even though we all knew it had already been made for us.

"Fine," Leighton choked out. "But I'm coming in to grab my pajamas."

She pushed past Nellie, who was too busy sizing me up like an overprotective parent. "I'm trusting you with her," she told me, the warning in her voice clear.

"I'm not going to try anything."

"Oh, Killian. Don't disappoint me like that," she said cryptically before leaving me alone in the hall, wondering what the fuck just happened. I didn't have too much time to mull it over. Leighton trudged out of her room, arms full of clothing, and brushed by me into my room. *Our* room. *Holy shit.*

I'm going to need a long shower tonight.

A while later, after we'd both changed—her into those ridiculously tiny shorts and an oversized T-shirt that left little to the imagination, me into a clean pair of boxer briefs—and I'd rubbed one out in the shower, we met beside the bed.

"So . . . ," I trailed off, offering her the chance to take the lead.

"So . . ."

"So, we should probably talk about what happened," she blew out in one breath. At the same time, I asked, "So, what side of the bed do you prefer?"

We both smiled. "Talk about what?" I asked her. I knew perfectly well what she was talking about, but I wanted to hear her say it.

"The kiss, killjoy," she blurted out. She lowered her voice and added, "You kissed me."

"You kissed me back."

She leveled me with a glare. "That . . . was . . ." I waited while she searched for an excuse. I bit back a smile. It was good to know I hadn't been the only one affected by our kiss. "That was *because* my parents were watching."

I nodded. "Right."

"It's true."

"No, I sleep on the *right* side of the bed."

I pointed toward my well-worn pillow. Her cheeks flushed.

"Oh."

"Is that okay?"

She shrugged. "It's your bed."

We were quiet after that. When we got into our respective sides of the bed. When I turned off the bedside lamp. When she repositioned the extra pillows between us to form a barricade of sorts. Her breathing slowed as the scenarios ran rampant through my brain. I thought the orgasm in the shower might relieve me, settle me, but no such luck.

I thought she might've fallen asleep, until I heard her whisper, "We can't let that happen again."

"Sure, princess."

"I'm serious," she said defensively, clutching the blankets to her chest. Something told me she was trying to convince herself more than me. "It'll only make things messy. Messier than they already are. *This* isn't real."

I rolled to my side, away from her, lest I give away the smile on my face and the growing erection in my Jockeys.

"Sure, princess."

Chapter Five

December 15th

Leighton

Today began the same as the previous three days: with me waking up long before my morning alarm, back plastered to Killian's front, close enough to feel his thick, engorged cock pressing against me. I should've known the behemoth would have a dick to match. And for the third day in a row, it took everything in me to stealthily slither out of his ridiculously soft sheets, rather than stay in bed and put that dick to use.

It would be so easy to just slip my panties aside and . . .

"Nope," I said aloud.

"Geez," Nellie groused from behind me, her voice thick with sleep. "I just wanted coffee."

"That I can do." I'd finally mastered Killian's fancy-pants coffee maker.

I turned to hand my sister a mug and found her in a surprising state of disarray. The time difference combined with yesterday's trip to

Santa Monica's Christkindlmarket must've really taken a toll because generally, she rose with the sun and was dressed before breakfast. I liked this side of her, though. It reminded me that she was more than the "practically perfect in every way" Disney princess my parents painted her out to be. She was human, just like the rest of us, morning breath and all.

"So, how did you sleep?" Nellie arched her brow suggestively.

"Good," I answered coldly. I wasn't lying, though, and just admitting that soured my caffeine buzz. The truth was, I didn't want to acknowledge that I'd slept more soundly the last few nights in Killian's bed than I had in months. I didn't want to think about how much I enjoyed his touch, in and out of bed. And I definitely didn't want to discuss my mounting attraction toward my fake fiancé. My fake fiancé who hadn't tried to kiss me or initiate anything physical beyond a harmless hair twirl or handhold in days.

Because I asked him not to. And he listened. Damn him for being so respectful of my boundaries.

Nellie clicked her tongue. "Such a waste."

"I don't want to hear it."

"I see the way you look at him."

"Nellie."

"And the way he looks at you."

"Nell—" *Wait a minute.* "How does he look at me?"

She smiled behind her coffee mug. "Like he'd tear your clothes off with his teeth and lick you like a Tootsie Pop, if you gave him a chance."

"Well," I croaked before clearing my suddenly dry throat. "That's an . . . idea."

"You could make it a reality."

I sighed, drumming my fingers on the edge of my mug. "Look, things are already complicated, to say the least. Mostly because of you, *dear* sister."

She flipped her hair over her shoulder. It sickened me how good her hair looked first thing in the morning. Between the two of us, only she had been blessed with the gene for naturally curly hair.

"I just want to get through the holidays physically and emotionally unscathed. Okay?"

"I hear you, loud and clear." She waited until my mouth was full of coffee before adding, "But couldn't you just use him for his body?"

"Works for me," a voice growled from behind me.

Coffee sputtered out of my mouth, soaking the countertop. A few stray droplets dribbled down my shirt, right between my breasts. I turned away from them both, my light-footed fake fiancé and my traitor of a sister. From where we'd been sitting at the kitchen island, there was no way she hadn't seen him coming down the stairs.

I'd just finished dabbing the coffee and spittle from beneath my top when I felt him behind me, still not touching me but just out of reach.

"You alright?" he asked.

I cleared my throat. "Just fine."

"Is there time for me to get a swim in before we go tree shopping?"

Somehow, we'd managed to convince my mother to hold off on tree shopping until today, the first day we'd both had off work since they arrived.

"Are you going to put on a bathing suit this time?" I winced, immediately realizing I'd revealed too much.

"Did you sneak a peek, princess?" I kept my mouth shut. Even though I was facing away from him, I could tell he was smiling. He leaned closer, his warm breath fanning my ear. "All you have to do is ask."

Please. I was five seconds away from asking him to bend me over this counter and fuck me sideways, my family and tree shopping be damned.

"Leia," my mother screeched from upstairs, "can you bring up the Lotronex in my purse? Your father's IBS is acting up."

Nothing killed the mood faster than mention of your parent's bowels.

I blew out a breath, reflexively dropping my head back. My eyes widened when I ran smack dab into a rock-hard chest. Killian's eyes sparkled with amusement, like I was some unexpected, precious gift. The answer to a question he'd been looking for.

At first, I thought he might kiss me. Upside-down, Tobey Maguire *Spider-Man* style. And I would have let him. Instead, he tilted his face down until his lips met the crown of my head. Not kissing me, just resting there.

"Come find me when you need me, princess."

And with that, he was gone. I waited until I heard the sliding door to the patio close behind him before slowly releasing my clutch on the countertop. It was the only thing holding me up at this point. My bottom half had turned to a gooey mess the moment he'd called me "princess."

"Sooo," Nellie said, startling me. I'd almost forgotten she was here. "How many licks does it take to get to the center of a Tootsie Pop?"

"Shut up," I grumbled. "Let's go buy a fucking tree."

"No, Hank. This one's all wrong." Mom's lips twisted as she carefully examined the umpteenth Douglas Fir of the day. "The needles aren't shiny enough."

I tucked my hands into my coat pockets. My boiling temperature was no match for the afternoon breeze. It had dropped almost ten degrees since we'd gotten to the tree farm two hours ago. While Mom had begrudgingly agreed to picking out a tree at the nearby tree lot, Dad had insisted that per tradition, he get to chop one down. Unbeknownst to the rest of us, he'd even packed his own axe.

How he'd gotten that through TSA, I'd never know.

And through it all, Killian had played the dutiful son-in-law. He'd carried the tree stand. He'd stood beside the Fraser Firs and Blue Spruces so my mother could decide if they were tall enough. He'd even fetched us all hot chocolate, which I'd promptly doctored with peppermint schnapps from my purse.

"Mom, we've been at this for two hours," Nellie moaned. "I'm cold, I'm hungry, and I have an important call at six p.m."

"About your test results? Did you pass? Are you a lawyer now?" I tried to contain my excitement. Just because law was so outside of my wheelhouse didn't mean I wasn't excited for Nell's accomplishments. That being said, I also didn't want to put any additional pressure on her.

"No . . . ," she answered, avoiding my eyes.

"Then what is it?"

"Don't worry about it."

What is she hiding? My sister wasn't one for secrets.

"Nell, what's going—"

"This is the one!" Mom shouted, loud enough for the entire tree farm to hear us. "Just look at him. He's so . . . majestic."

It was a fine-looking tree. A Noble Fir, with a thick, round bottom (just like me). And if we were going off Killian's height, it had to be at least seven feet tall.

"Rupert," Nellie suggested.

"Leopold." That was Dad.

Killian leaned over to ask, "What's happening?"

"We name the tree."

His brows lifted. "You name the . . ."

"The Christmas tree, yes. It's . . . tradition." I rolled my eyes.

"Walking in a Wheatley Wonderland?"

I couldn't contain my chuckle. "Exactly. Generally, we land on some sort of old-timey name. Theodore, Otis—"

"Walter!" Mom said.

"There you go."

He was quiet as my family continued to spit names like a diss track. I added one here and there, in between sips of my Peppermint Hot Schnapp-late, but none of them seemed to suit, according to Mom.

"By the way," I said, turning to Killian, "we're going to Nora's wrap party tonight."

"What?"

His eyes widened in . . . fear? That couldn't be right.

"The cast of her show is throwing a wrap party slash holiday shindig slash 'we got renewed for a second season' celebration, so we're going."

"I wasn't really planning on going anywhere tonight, and—"

I slapped my hands to his shoulders. "Three days with my family is a lot, and this is just the beginning. I. Need. This."

He swallowed. I had no idea what he was worried about. My family could survive an evening without us. Hell, now that we'd picked out the tree, Mom would have something to keep her busy, Nellie had her super-secret phone call, and Dad, well . . .

Somehow, he always had something and nothing to do, all at once.

"Okay," Killian said solemnly.

"Thank you."

"Chester."

I wrinkled my brow. "Who?"

"The tree." He nodded toward the new addition to the family. "How about Chester?" he offered, a little louder this time.

"Chester," Mom repeated, mulling it over. "We've never had a Chester before. Hank?"

Dad shrugged. "Works for me if it means I get to use my axe finally."

"Chester it is, then!" Mom cuddled up to Killian's side, placing her arm through his. "What an excellent suggestion, Killian."

"Uh, thank you." He grimaced. I was starting to get the feeling that he wasn't the biggest fan of attention, even though the spotlight clearly loved him. "It was my grandfather's name."

"Oh, lovely. Tell me all about him, hon."

He looked back at me, his eyes searching mine for some kind of excuse or escape, as my mother carted him away, arm-in-arm. Two things I knew to be true. First, there was no escaping Wanda Wheatley, no matter how hard you tried. I had thirty years of living proof. And second, we were going to be late for Nora's party tonight.

Killian

Until tonight, I thought sharing a bed with Leighton while not being able to touch her the way I wanted (hell, the way we both wanted) was my own metaphorical Hell.

I was wrong. This was worse.

A dark and crowded room, full of unfamiliar sounds and faces save for Bowie, Nora, and the woman beside me.

". . . but now we're going to Palm Springs, so do you want the house?" Bowie asked.

"Sorry, what?"

"We're spending New Year's Eve in Palm Springs," Bowie said. I could barely make him out over the music. "It was a last-minute gift from my folks. We had an Airbnb booked in Big Bear, though, that's nonrefundable. Do you want it?"

"Oh, well," I stammered, tugging on my collar, "I don't know."

His eyes flirted between Leighton and me. She and Nora were caught up in their own mouth-to-ear exchange beside us. Who the fuck chose EDM for an office holiday party?

"Seems like things are going well, yeah?"

I plastered on a grin. "They're going *somewhere*. I'm not sure where just yet."

"Maybe to Big Bear?" He winked. It was nice to know Leighton and I had his "blessing."

"We'll see," I croaked. I could feel my temperature rising by the second. My pulse was already out of control.

"You alright, mate?" Bowie clapped a hand on my shoulder, but his touch reverberated through my body. A resounding echo of pain. He was practically yelling over the noise and yet, sounded miles away. Even now, I could feel the warehouse walls beginning to close in.

"I just . . . It's all . . . too much." *Fuck, I can't even talk.*

Judging by his grim expression, I could tell he knew what was coming. I'd known Bowie for going on two decades, and during that time, he'd witnessed a fair share of my anxiety attacks. He knew the signs, was well aware of my stressors. Which was probably why he'd been so surprised to see me at tonight's festivities. I'd declined Nora's invite over a week ago, but unfortunately, I hadn't shared that with Leighton. Worse, I also hadn't shared my history of anxiety with her. I didn't know why, exactly. There'd been plenty of opportunities. But the last thing I wanted to do was ruin any headway we'd made over the last few weeks.

In my heart, I knew she wouldn't care. In fact, she'd probably be pissed that I'd kept it from her. But, as per usual, my head and heart were feuding. Which was why I was currently running scenarios and drowning out Bowie's comforting words.

Scenario A: Get the fuck out of this room. By any means possible. Easier said than done. After a brief faculties check, I concluded that my feet were pretty much molded to the ground. *Great, we're entering Stage Two.*

Scenario B: Burn the place to the ground.

Scenario C: Call for . . .

"I told you, Nora. The answer is no."

I swiveled my head, focusing my narrowing-by-the-second tunnel vision on Leighton, who despite wearing jeans was still the most stunning woman in the room.

"Please. I need that dress in my life." Nora clasped her hands together in front of her. "I haven't been able to stop thinking about it since you showed me the sketch."

"Okay, I did not show it to you," Leighton argued. "You rifled through my desk."

"Sure, sure. Bo, did you know you had such a talented friend?" Nora pulled Bowie closer to her side. "She designs clothes."

"I didn't know that, and I'd love to hear more about it, but I think Kill might need me—"

I tuned them out completely. Next thing I knew, there were multiple sets of hands wrapped around my side leading me farther and farther away from the music. In between steps, I made out a word or two. "Anxiety," "noise," and "panic," to name a few. *All of my favorites.* I didn't know how long we walked or where we were going. I didn't care, so long as I got out of that stuffy, crowded room.

Eventually, a cool hand on my cheek made me stir. "Killjoy?"

The haze began to dissipate. Everything started to come back into focus, starting with the realization that I was now outside—perhaps in the parking lot or side of the building—and ending with the startling discovery that Leighton was squatting beside me, running her fingers through my hair.

"It's okay," she whispered calmly, bathing me in reassurances. "Everything's okay. You're safe."

My eyes traced over her brows, down her flushed cheeks, and around the curve of her lips. The *thump-thump* against my hand clued me into the fact that Leighton was holding my hand to her chest.

I must've shown some trepidation because she added, "Bowie said feeling my heartbeat might help. He and Nora went to get our coats." She reached for something at her side, an uncapped, plastic water bottle. "Here, drink this."

I used my free hand to sip the water. With the other, I counted Leighton's heartbeats, paying no mind to the way her breasts sandwiched my hand. There was nothing sexual about this. Leighton's fingers continued combing waves through my loose locks. It felt so good, so safe. I refrained from leaning into her touch, from moaning aloud the way I wanted to.

"Is this helping? Is there anything else I can do?"

"No, you're perfect." *Smooth.* Her cheeks flushed at my Freudian slip. "*This* is perfect."

Before I knew it, I was draining the final drops of water from the bottle. I set it aside but made no move to extricate my hand from hers. She monitored my face for any signs of distress, waiting until she presumably found none before asking, "Why didn't you tell me? I feel like being prone to anxiety attacks is something your partner should know about you, don't you think?"

"I didn't want you to think of me any differently."

A wounded look crossed her face. "You thought I would?"

"People have before." I shrugged then added, "But no, I didn't think you would."

The corner of her lips turned up.

"Why didn't you tell me you design clothes?"

"You heard that?" This time, she was the one trying to pull her hand from mine. I didn't let her go.

"I did."

She sighed. "It was a long time ago." I lifted my brows, waiting. "But yes, in my previous life, for a *very* brief time, I went to fashion school."

"That's brilliant." I meant it. I envied creatives, the same way I was sure some of them envied athletes or scientists or mathematicians. I'd never know, never understand how Leighton's brain worked that way. Just another reason to add to my list.

Reason #71: Her creativity.

Right behind *Reason #70: She was there when I needed her.*

"I'm glad *you* think so." She smiled sadly.

"It does seem like something a partner should know about you, don't you think?" I asked, throwing her words back at her. "What if your parents mentioned it? Or your sister?"

She snorted, as if the very idea were unbelievable. "Trust me, they won't." She shrugged. "I dropped out after a year."

"Do you still do it?"

"No," she said, confused. "I dropped out."

"You don't have to have a degree to design clothes."

Her mouth opened and shut, almost as if she had never considered the possibility. I wasn't an expert on the fashion industry by any means, but was that so far-fetched?

"I wanted to, um . . . I mean . . ." She fumbled her words. Despite her clear discomfort, there was something refreshing about seeing her so out of sorts, so unrehearsed. "I wanted to design for bigger bodies, like mine. And at the time, that wasn't really an option."

I blinked. "So said who?"

"So said my adviser. And my teachers. And my classmates." She stopped. This time, I pulled her hand to my chest. Her eyes traced the movement before climbing up to meet my own. She didn't fight me. "I know I probably should've just said, 'fuck 'em all,' and made my clothes anyway, the way I wanted, for the people I wanted, but it's hard when it feels like nobody supports you or sees the things you see. That, and I was a dumb nineteen-year-old kid on my own in a new city. So, it just seemed easier to call it and move on."

"I get that." I let her go and climbed to my feet. When I didn't immediately tip over, I offered her my hand to help her up, too. Thankfully, this attack had been far less severe than others I'd experienced. Already, my heart had nearly returned to its normal resting rate. "But just so you know, I think you can do anything you want. And I'm here to help you do that. *If* you want my help."

She nudged the ground with her toe self-consciously, leaning into the brick wall beside us. "Thank you."

Somewhere nearby, a door opened, releasing another swarm of partygoers. I leaned my body against the bricks, bringing us nearly shoulder to shoulder. Close enough for me to see our breaths intermingling in the frigid air but farther than I'd prefer.

"I feel like a dick, by the way." Her statement made my eyes pop. *Where did that come from?* "I never would've asked you to come here tonight if I knew it would be too much."

Ah, got it.

"That's okay." I took a shot and draped my arm around her shoulders, drawing her closer. "Besides, spending the evening alone with your family would've probably been too much, too."

And just like that, the tension she'd been holding slipped away, her shoulders dropped back into place, and her laughter filled any remaining cracks in my armor.

I was unexpectedly woken up later that night, mere hours after returning from the party, by Leighton's pert ass rubbing against my dick. At first, I thought she was dreaming. Hell, I thought I was dreaming because I'd spent countless nights envisioning this very scenario. And yet, here it was, playing out in real time.

A quick glance at the bedside table told me it was a little after two a.m. When we'd come home prematurely from the party, her family had already retired for the night. We'd gone about our pre-bed routine and fallen asleep a little after midnight.

Which meant that sometime in the past two hours, Leighton had gone from safely sleeping on her side of my spacious California King to plastering her lush backside up against my now rock-hard front, riding my cock like it was her own personal Hippity Hop. Already, I could feel the heat of her pussy soaking through her boxers, onto my briefs. I'd enshrine them in gold tomorrow if it meant preserving her pussy juices for all eternity. Just thinking about it had my cock twitching, ready to rip through the layers between us.

"Princess," I groaned into her neck when she ground her ass against me once more, this time a little harder. "What are you doing?"

"I can't help it," she breathed. "It feels too good."

My hand stilled the movement of her hips. She moaned in protest. I needed to make sure we were on the same page, that she knew exactly what she was doing and who she was doing it with.

"What happened to not letting things get messy?"

"I like messy," she said. The smile she shot me over her shoulder made my cock ache.

You little minx. She didn't realize the switch she'd just triggered. I tilted my head down so she could see me clearer in the dark.

"You want to get messy with me, princess?" I ran my fingers from her hip down the soft rolls of her belly, inching underneath the band of her boxer shorts. She shivered in response.

"I just want to feel good."

"Who do you want to make you feel good?" When she didn't answer, I wrapped my other hand, the one not closing in on her clit around the length of her throat. Not squeezing, just hard enough to hold her head in place, to keep her where I wanted her when I repeated my question. "Who, princess?"

Her eyes sparkled with excitement and maybe a hint of trepidation. She should be scared. Not of me, but rather of the things I made her feel. I should know; she terrified the shit out of me for that very reason. "You, Killian."

"Say it again."

"I want you to make me feel good."

My mouth met hers, swallowing her moan at the very moment my hand slipped south to cover her pussy. I dipped one finger inside her, swirling it through her juices before adding another. This time, when I pulled them out, I circled her clit, drawing some of her natural lube around the distended nub. Her mouth broke away from mine.

"Killian," she gasped.

"I love it when you say my name."

My lips traced a path down her neck, leaving wet kisses along the way. She whimpered when I nipped the spot just behind her ear, then she moaned when I lavished it with my tongue.

Hansel left breadcrumbs. I left love bites.

I didn't know what had changed her mind or why this was happening tonight of all nights, but I wasn't going to waste this opportunity to leave my mark. To make her mine.

My fingers pistoned in and out of her, matching rhythm with her breathy moans. When I added a third finger, she groaned into my bicep.

"Careful, princess," I murmured against her neck. "Wouldn't want to wake Mom and Dad." Her pussy tightened in response. I smiled at the hitch in her breath. Apparently, Leighton was an exhibitionist of sorts. I was all for exploring that later, after I made her come.

She ground her pussy against my hand, desperate for release. "That's it. Fuck my fingers like a good girl."

"God, Killian . . ."

Her hips jerked forward reflexively. "I'm so close."

It wouldn't be long now. She was racing towards the edge, and I was more than willing to send her over. All it took was a few more strokes and a pinch of her clit to send her soaring. My lips met hers just in time to swallow her cries. I locked my arm around her front, holding her in place while she rode out the waves of pleasure.

When her hips finally stopped undulating, I slowly removed my fingers from the warm depths of her cunt and brought them to my lips. She bit her lip when I put them in my mouth and proceeded to lick them clean.

Mmm. Best cream I'd ever tasted. I licked my lips like a satisfied cat.

"I should, um . . . ," she stammered, trying to catch her breath. Her self-consciousness had returned. "Maybe we should—"

"Go to sleep, princess," I growled, my voice tinged with desire. My cock was still painfully hard, but that was nothing new when it came to Leighton. "We should go to sleep."

"But you're still—"

"Trust me," I said into her neck. Her pulse was still beating raggedly. "I'll survive."

I wanted nothing more than to roll her over and sink inside her, but she wasn't ready for that. She was more than a one-night stand, a random fuck from a bar or dating app. I'd had a year to realize what she meant to me, but she hadn't had the same. She was only just now coming around to the idea of us being something more than friends, or friends of friends even.

I didn't want to be just the fake fiancé who finger-fucked her one Christmas. I wanted to be her forever.

"Don't you want me to . . ." She jutted her ass against my throbbing cock. I used the hand still in her boxers to lightly slap her pussy, making her entire body jump.

"Princess, it's too late and we are too tired for me to *begin* to share the list of things I want you to do to me. Besides, your parents are right down the hall, and frankly, the first time I'm inside you, I want to be able to hear you scream." I punctuated my statement with another nip to her neck. "So, for now, let's go to sleep."

She settled back in my arms, not a trace of space between us. After a few minutes, she whispered, "Can I at least go back to my side of the bed?"

She just had to have the last word. Who was I kidding? I wouldn't have it any other way.

"No," I said, drawing a hand through her hair. "You're right where you belong."

Chapter Six

December 16th

Leighton

I felt it before I opened my eyes. Searing pain blazed through my lower abdomen, which could only mean one thing.

Fuck.

"Princess," Killian said, his voice an octave lower than usual. Damn, even his morning voice was sexy as fuck. He ran a gentle hand over my side. "I don't want to alarm you, but I think you started your period."

"Fuck." I shot up like a cannon, immediately regretting it when a pang of nausea struck. "I'm so sorry. I have PCOS and I don't usually get a period, but when I do, it's bad. Like, can't get out of bed, can barely keep my head up, bad." The words spewed out of me like vomit, which, speaking of . . .

I threw off the blankets, wincing when I noticed the splotch of red on the sheets. There was no time to be embarrassed. I made a mad dash for the attached bath, threw the door closed behind me, dropped to my knees in front of the toilet, and lost my lunch, or rather, last night's dinner.

When nothing but dry heaves racked my body, I got back to my feet and groaned. This wasn't good. Retching and standing had already sapped what little energy I had, and I'd just woken up.

After brushing my teeth—with water only because there was no doubt in my mind that my minty toothpaste would make me gag—and splashing some cool water on my face, I opened the door.

There he was, halfway through changing out the bloody sheets on his bed. Another stabbing pain pierced my gut. This time, I couldn't tell if it was just another cramp or if my competency kink had been engaged.

Maybe both.

"I'll just be a minute," he said, barely looking up from the bed. How was he this unbothered? It should be a crime for him to look this good first thing in the morning. He'd thrown his hair up in his usual bun, and he was still wearing his boxer briefs from the night before. Only now, they were dotted in . . .

"Oh my god!"

"What?" he asked, genuinely concerned.

"I . . ." I couldn't even bring myself to say it. Instead, I waved my hand wildly toward his crotch. "I . . . on you." He looked down at himself. "Oh my god, I can't even look at you right now."

"Princess."

"No," I said, covering my face with my hands. Janelle was the one who believed in manifestation, but maybe if I willed it hard enough, I'd disappear altogether.

"Leighton," he said, this time from right in front of me. When had he crossed the room? He pulled my hands away from my face, threading my fingers through his own. "We've been over this. I'm not afraid of a little blood."

"It's a lot of blood."

He kissed my forehead. I basked in the tickling feeling of his overgrown whiskers against my skin. Only for a moment though. I was too uncomfortable to enjoy his touch. I wasn't lying when I told him my periods were bad, thanks to my PCOS. Cramps, nausea, loss of appetite. It fucking sucked. But I also had fifteen years of experience on how to manage it. The timing was inconvenient, though. Bowie would cover for me at work, I knew that, but what was I going to do about my family?

"What do you need?"

"To go back in time, wake up before you, and clean up this mess before you found it?" I asked into his bare chest, still too embarrassed to look him in the eyes.

He took the choice away from me by using his fingers to tilt my chin up, until my eyes met his. "Please, baby. Let me help you. What do you need?"

I bit down on my lip before answering. "I'm going to take a shower, but after that, I really am going to be worthless."

"Never."

I smiled. "What I mean is, I have no idea what to do about my family. When I get my period, I'm down for the count. Bed, couch, shower, that's it. We have a week until Christmas, I've barely started my shopping, and now this? There's not going to be enough time to—"

"Breathe, baby." I sucked in a deep breath. This was a PCOS side effect I'd never experienced before: oversharing. I had a feeling that had more to do with the nearly naked man rubbing his hands down my arms than it did with my uterus.

It also didn't escape me that he'd called me "baby" twice now. And truth be told, I wasn't sure if I liked it.

I prefer "princess."

"That's good to know," he said smugly, smiling from ear to ear.

My cheeks burned. Apparently, I'd said that last part aloud.

"I'll stick to 'princess' for now. In the meantime, why don't you jump in the shower while I finish changing the sheets?"

"But my family?"

"I'll take care of them, too."

"But—"

He planted his lips on mine, swallowing whatever excuse I'd been cooking up. This kiss was different from our others. Slow, lazy. It wasn't a prelude to anything more. No, this kiss was the main event, the whole damn show.

When he was satisfied that he'd kissed the excuses out of me, he pulled back, dropped one more peck on my forehead, and turned me toward the bathroom.

I took my time in Killian's shower, or what I'd aptly named, *the glass palace*. The thing was huge, taking up nearly half of the en suite. It also came complete with a steam setting and a bench on either end of the rainfall showerhead over top. This was a shower made for . . . activities. And while I wasn't opposed to said activities during my period—in fact, there was nothing I wanted more than a continuation of our midnight hook up—I barely had it in me to stand up right now.

Eventually, I dragged my ass out of the shower and back to our bed. *Wait.* When had I started thinking of it as our bed? *Fuck.* My mind was racing; my stomach was doing somersaults. So much had changed between us in the last few weeks, and that was nothing compared to the last twenty-four hours. He'd opened up about his history with anxiety, and I'd shared my decade-old insecurities about dropping out of college. I'd even showed him the design Nora had mentioned when we'd gotten home last night.

Last night. *Oh, boy.*

And then this morning. *Oh, boy.*

Same sentiment, different tone.

I didn't want to think about it. I didn't want to play back every kiss, touch, and tease, at least that was what I kept telling myself. So, I did what any grown ass woman hiding from her feelings would do: I climbed back into bed, tucked my face into Killian's pillow, and fell back asleep.

I was startled awake sometime later by the sweet aroma of chocolate, peanut butter, and potato chips? It almost smelled like . . .

No. It can't be, can it?

It didn't take long to get my answer. After a few seconds, just long enough for me to sit up and stack a mountain of pillows behind, Killian strode through the bedroom door, a tray in his hands. The man was a goddamn domestic wet dream.

He set the tray down beside me, grinning when he noticed I'd taken up residence on *his* side of the bed.

"Did you . . . ? Are those . . . ?"

"I asked your sister what you liked. Apparently, these are your favorites," he said, gesturing to the plate of cookies on the tray.

Not cookies, bars. *PMS Bars.*

The ooey-gooiest, most life-changing, most orgasmic creation I'd ever enjoyed. Killian himself was a close second. They were the perfect concoction of graham crackers, M&Ms, peanut butter chips, and pretzels, because nothing soothed my uterus more than the salty-sweet combination.

"I can't believe you made these."

"It wasn't that hard." He handed me a square. *Dear god, they're still warm.*

"Still, you didn't need to do that."

He cocked his head to the side. "Princess, I don't know what kind of people you've been with, but taking care of you when you're not feeling well is the bare fucking minimum."

When I took my first bite, my eyes practically rolled back in my head. Judging by the darkening of Killian's eyes, I may have audibly moaned. It was safe to say he was envisioning my mouth wrapped around something else. I knew I was. That was another charming side effect of my period. Constant horniness. Peak levels of feeling like hot, wet garbage while also wanting to . . . stuff *my* hot, wet garbage in somebody's mouth.

"So," Killian said, startling me out of my graphic visions of blow jobs and trash cans—a combination I never thought would cross my mind. "What else can I do to make you more comfortable?"

"I already told you." I covered my mouth while I finished chewing. "You don't need to do anything."

"And I already told you I'm here to help. So, please . . ." He paused, placing his hand over mine. His warm, callused fingers gave me goose-bumps. "Let me."

I'd just finished swallowing when a new thought occurred. "What happened to my parents?"

"Oh, they're halfway to Disneyland by now."

"What?"

"Yeah, I booked them two nights at the Grand California. Bought them park-hopper tickets, the whole VIP package. Janelle, too. Your mom is very excited to have breakfast with Minnie Mouse."

Oh. My. God.

Mom's Minnie Mouse collection was the sole reason why Nellie and I had shared a bedroom growing up. To this day, my parents' third bedroom functioned as a shrine to the beloved cartoon rodent.

"Killian, that's too much. I can't—"

"I can. So, please, let me." He smoothed a hand through my hair. It probably looked like a mussed mess, and yet, from the way Killian looked at me, you'd think it was plated in gold. "It's only a couple of days. And I . . ."

He hesitated.

I hadn't meant to make him feel guilty or uncomfortable in any way. I rolled his hand over with mine, lacing my fingers through his. He was doing so much to make a safe space for me. At the very least, I owed him the same. When his eyes met mine, I smiled, encouraging him to continue.

"We all have different ways to show we care. I know it might seem like I'm just throwing money—"

"Not at all. That was very sweet of you." I nibbled my lip. "Between the house, the decorations, Disneyland. I just never want you to feel like that's what *this* is."

His lips curved up, understanding washing over him. "Believe me, princess. I know that's not what *this* is. Okay?"

"Okay."

"Good."

"Great."

My attention shifted to our interlocked hands. For the next few minutes, we sat in comfortable silence. I memorized the pattern of his freckles, and he traced the inch-long scar between my thumb and forefinger, a sewing machine mishap from my first month at college. I couldn't get over how much I'd misjudged this man, how little I'd thought of him just because he was a public figure with a hefty wallet.

Shame on me. But complicated as it might be, there was no denying the connection between us now.

Fuck, this was my Elizabeth Bennet moment. And this was his Mr. Darcy hand flex.

"I'll ask you again, princess," he said finally, drawing my hand into his lap and rubbing his thumb over my wrist. I'd never thought of the wrist as an erogenous zone. It never had been with any of my previous partners, but with Killian . . . "Now that we have the place to ourselves for the next two days, what can I do to make you more comfortable?"

"Well." I paused, for nothing other than dramatic effect. "There is one thing that always helps."

His eyes sparkled with anticipation. As much as I wanted to take advantage of every filthy, fucked-up fantasy scrolling through his brain (and mine), I had something a little different in mind. Something far more relaxing that required a lot less strenuous movement.

"Want to get high?"

Killian

I was fourteen the first time I got high.

Bowie and I smoked a joint behind the local market, ate our weight in crisps, and then ran back to his house where we confessed every last detail to his mums. The whole experience had soured my taste for experimenting with marijuana, at least for a few years.

By the time I reached uni, football had become my main priority, a way out of my small town and even smaller community. I wasn't going to let anything interfere with my future, and that included alcohol, drugs, and sex, though I admit, I was more liberal with the latter.

Fast forward to now, me sitting on the floor of my bedroom, head between my fake fiancée's thighs, stoned out of my mind, nibbling on my fourth (or maybe fifth) PMS bar while she braided my hair. This was a high I hoped I'd never come down from.

"You can't be serious," Leighton said from behind me, laughter mingling with her words.

"I am."

"*Murder, She Wrote*."

"Yes."

"That's your favorite show?"

"Absolutely."

It wasn't the first time I'd gotten this reaction. But how was I to blame for the world's poor taste in television programs?

"She's got a quality selection of sweaters and vests; I'll give you that. But what makes you a *Murder, She Wrote* stan?"

"I love a good mystery."

"Sweater vests and mysteries?" She playfully tugged on my hair, unlocking a new kink. "That's it?"

I chuckled. "No, there's more. I met Angela Lansbury when I was a kid."

"Wait, really?"

"Yeah." I swallowed. "It's one of the first memories I have, actually. I was nine, I think. Mum was working in this flower shop and the owner's daughter was cast in a musical in the West End. She was so chuffed, she gave all her employees tickets for Christmas that year. Mum and I took the bus into London for the matinee. Four hours each way. And when we went to meet the boss's daughter after the show, she introduced us to the star herself, Ms. Angela Lansbury. I've been a diehard *stan*, as you say, ever since."

Leighton's giggles echoed throughout the room. I felt one final hair pull, followed by the sound of something snapping into place, before she announced, "There. What do you think?"

I held up the hot-pink hand mirror she'd given me. Two intricately woven braids now decorated my head, one on either side, a perfect match. "Stunning."

"She sounds great."

"We only spoke for about ten seconds, but—"

"No." She paused. The tone of her voice shifted to something much more somber. "Your mom."

My eyes met hers in the mirror. "She was," I said softly.

"Four hours on a bus. Each way." She sighed. "Not every mother would do that for their child."

"I was lucky to have her."

She held my gaze. "And she was lucky to have you, too."

We were crossing into unexplored territory. I could feel it happening, another seismic shift in our relationship. We'd experienced several of them, of varying stages, ever since the day she'd moved in. And somehow, a part of me knew this one would be different. A part of me knew there would be no going back after this.

I set the mirror aside and turned to face her, resting my hands on her thighs. It was an unfamiliar feeling, looking up at somebody for a change. But it was important to me that she felt safe, that she knew she had all the physical and emotional leverage for what came next.

"Can I ask, what's the issue between you and your mum?"

She blinked. "I don't know if I'm high enough to talk about that."

"Please."

"It's complicated."

"I've got time."

There was no rush for her to answer. Nowhere to be, nobody waiting on us. For the first time in weeks, it was just us. Princess and killjoy. Just the way I wanted it, and just the thing she'd spent a year trying to avoid.

She straightened her shoulders. "My parents are both from Ohio."

"Right." It was more than clear she was just getting started.

"My grandparents are from Ohio. My great-grandparents are from Ohio. Every single Wheatley aunt, uncle, cousin, niece, nephew, they are *all* from Ohio. Not only that," she said, jumping to her feet. The wince on her face told me that despite the weed and peanut butter treats, she was still in pain.

She sat back down. "Not only that, but I come from a long line of blue-collar farmers, builders, and heterosexuals. And as you might've noticed, I am none of those."

"Janelle isn't either," I pointed out.

"Janelle is, to the best of my knowledge, straight as an arrow. She also graduated from college *and* law school, *and* still lives within a four-mile radius of at least six family members." The words whooshed out of her, along with a couple of tears. "And look, it's not that I think they love her more than me or that they favor her. I just wish . . . I wish they spent more time getting to know me and less trying to turn me into them. I'm tired of feeling like every choice I make is a disappointment."

By the time she finished, tears were coursing down her cheeks. I stood up on my knees, bringing my face nearly even with hers. "They're not disappointed in you," I told her, wiping the moisture from her face. "They just don't understand."

"Well, they should support me either way."

"I agree."

"And it's not *just* my mom." She sniffled. "She's just easier to blame, I guess, because she does most of the talking. I feel like shit even saying that aloud because I know that's not fair to her either."

Another sob racked her body.

I'd never given much thought to having children of my own, mostly because of my less-than-ideal upbringing. But I had no doubt that it was an impossible feat, especially for mothers. Fathers, on the other hand, got off too easily, in my opinion. That was what happened, though, when you lived in a society that had unrealistic expectations for women and next to none for men.

I tucked her head into the crook of my neck, stroking my hand up and down her back, soothing her while she cried. Her revelation put a lot of things into perspective: her fears about sharing her designs, her reluctance to accept help, even from the people closest to her. She didn't want to disappoint them.

She didn't want them to love her any less.

When her breathing finally evened out, I told her, "Whether they realize it or not, they're very lucky to have you, Leighton." She paused when I used her name. "I know you probably don't want to hear this, *and* maybe I'm a bastard for saying it, but I think you're lucky to have them, too."

She pulled back then. *Great. Now I'm the disappointment.* Her quivering chin would have sent me to my knees if I wasn't already there. Leighton was one of the strongest people I knew. The last thing I wanted was to see her crumble.

"I know they drive you mad and they haven't always supported you the way you need, the way you *deserve*, but at least they're there." Her face fell, utterly guilt stricken. "And I promise, I'm not trying to play the 'woe is me' orphan card. I'm not trying to invalidate your feelings. However much you decide to include your family in your life is entirely up to you, and I'll support you. I just thought you should know. I think you're all very lucky to have each other. And I'm lucky to have you, too."

Her eyes widened. Fearing that I might have laid out all my cards too soon, I quickly added, "Er, for a little while, at least."

Her shoulders slouched. Was she disappointed by the thought of our arrangement being temporary? Neither of us had been brave enough to broach the subject, but it was only a matter of time. Now that I'd kissed her, held her, talked her through her orgasm, there was no going back.

"Let's watch *Murder, She Wrote.*"

I tilted my head. "Sorry?"

"I'm done wallowing in self-pity, at least for today." She dried her eyes with the sleeve of my hoodie. The same one I'd lent her days ago that she'd yet to return to me. "I want to cuddle and watch *Murder, She Wrote.*"

I snorted. "Cuddles and cannabis?"

"And kissing."

"Yeah?" I tried to contain my excitement.

"But that's it." Her meaning was clear: no sex. She fidgeted nervously with her sleeves. "Are you okay with making out on the couch like teenagers while watching a forty-year-old mystery show?"

I hated that she even had to ask, as if cuddling and kissing her wasn't the highest of honors.

"I can't think of anything I'd enjoy more."

Chapter Seven

December 21st

Leighton

It was official: I was falling for my fake fiancé.

Over the past week, a *period*—pun intended—I would forever refer to as PCO*Sex*, Killian and I had fooled around in just about every room of the house. In between the bouts of piercing pain and nausea, that was.

We made out whenever we had the opportunity, stealing kisses in the laundry room during my family's Hallmark Christmas movie marathon and in the garage while my dad helped hang the outdoor lights. He felt me up in the kitchen while I made my morning coffee. We dry-humped on the couch like teenagers after everybody went to bed. We even graduated to some under-the-clothes action just yesterday, when I even let him use my vibrator on me until I came, screaming into his chest. We might've been fake engaged, but we were already cruising through the honeymoon phase full force.

However, our connection was much more than strictly sexual. We cuddled on the hammock out back, studying the stars and each other's physical and emotional scars. He shared enough stories about him and Bowie growing up together to give me a lifetime of blackmail on them both. I also found out firsthand that he was one hell of a teammate for Pictionary. The latter was good to know because as I had already explained to him, Christmas with the Wheatleys culminated in a series of holiday-themed minute-to-win-it games.

God help us. Everyone.

And through every bit of it—the cuddling, the not-suit-able-for-work action, the excessive family bonding—he cracked open another piece of my hard, protective shell. The barrier I had built years ago to protect myself.

"Leigh, you almost ready to go?" Janelle asked from somewhere in the living room. Despite the mass of wrapped gifts already under the tree, Mom had insisted on one final shopping trip for stocking stuffers, minute-to-win-it prizes, etc. Killian and Bowie were taking my dad golfing down in El Segundo.

"Just about."

I loaded the final dish from breakfast into the dishwasher and closed the door. Dad had whipped up his famous sausage and egg casserole for us, reminding me that my dad's cooking was one of the few things I missed about Ohio. Mom was the baker in the family, but Dad was the chef. If it didn't have sugar, chocolate, or pastry dough, it was Dad's domain.

Janelle wandered into the kitchen, dressed and ready to go. "What are we looking for exactly?"

"Well, Mom is looking for stocking stuffers and who knows what else," I answered sardonically. "I need to find something to wear to Killian's team party."

"What's the theme again?"

"Christmas Carol-oke."

The name alone made me cringe. From the sound of it, Killian's soccer captains would get along great with my mother. They had a whole host of activities planned for the team's holiday shindig, including Christmas karaoke.

"That sounds like fun!" I shook my head. Unlike me, Nellie had inherited the Wheatley holiday gene. Just one more thing that endeared her to my parents.

Nope, we're not going there.

Ever since my drug-induced heart-to-heart with Killian, I'd tried to lighten up on my parents. Not because my feelings were unfounded, but rather, I figured it would be much easier to change *my* frame of mind than change anything about my parents.

Something else had changed over the last few days, something that I thought I had left behind. I started drawing again. It started the day we got high. I'd walked past the sketch I'd left lying out, the one Nora had obsessed over. Next thing I knew, I had cozied up by the fire, sketchpad and pencils in hand. He hadn't asked questions, hadn't goaded me into showing him what I was working on. He simply plied me with charcuterie spreads—the man knew his way around a baked brie—and let me do my thing. But there was one thing he hadn't let me do.

Touch him.

Sure, I'd stroked his chest, braided his hair, and used his body to make myself come, more than once. But every time, he'd made it all about me. Every stroke, every poke, all me.

But my period had ended yesterday, and today, I was hankering for a handful of Killian cock.

Which was why when I heard the en suite shower turn on moments later, I excused myself.

"Be right back."

I didn't stop when Janelle called after me. I didn't stop until I reached the closed door to the attached bathroom Killian and I shared. When I opened it, steam rolled out, flooding the bedroom and momentarily obscuring my view.

And what a view it was.

My eyes traveled over him, starting from the length of his chestnut hair, darker than usual due to the water, down his tattooed torso, pausing to admire how the suds cascaded over and around each individual ab muscle, until finally, I zeroed on his very impressive, uncut dick.

Sans piercing.

Yes, that was right. Sadly, there would be no Prince Albert for Princess Leighton.

And surprisingly, I wasn't disappointed in the least. Because like just about everything else Killian-related, reality exceeded any preconceived expectations or fantasies.

"See something you like?"

My eyes shot up to meet his, full of amusement. He'd totally caught me peeking and for once, I wasn't the least bit embarrassed.

"It's not quite what I imagined," I teased, "but I suppose it'll do."

He lifted a brow, clearly picking up on the challenge in my voice. And judging the way his cock jumped, he appreciated it. He was growing harder by the second.

"Yeah?" He wrapped a hand around the base of his shaft, slowly sliding it up and down, never taking his eyes off mine. "You've thought about my cock?" I liked this side of Killian, the dirty-talking Dom that only came out to play when I engaged my inner brat.

I nodded but didn't give him any more than that. Not yet. Teasing him was too much fun.

"You gonna offer me a hand, princess?"

"I'm better with my mouth actually."

That shut him up. The hand on his cock froze when I tugged my long-sleeve off over my head. I could've sworn I heard him growl when I removed my bra. He'd done a lot of touching over the past week, but I'd never been topless in front of him. He moaned when I removed the rest of my clothes, giving him his first unencumbered look at my naked body. Knowing that he loved my body—every dip, curve, and wrinkle—made me feel all warm and tingly inside. But we were just getting started. Things were about to get a whole lot warmer.

"Move over."

He opened the glass door for me, and I stepped into the stall, immediately crowding him against the wall, away from the water's reach. He let me explore him, keeping his hands planted firmly on the curve of my hips. I could tell he wanted to do some exploring of his own, but he refrained. This was my show. There was something so powerful about topping from the bottom, so to speak. There was no doubt about who, between the two of us, had the upper hand when it came to sex. So, the fact that he was letting me lead this time around meant something.

When my hand dropped to the root of his cock, he tilted his head back, opening his mouth to vocalize his pleasure.

"You like that?" I asked, running my tongue around his nipple.

"You know I do." He grunted.

I kissed my way down his body, wincing slightly when my knees connected harshly with the hard shower floor. *Fucking river rocks.*

"Wait," Killian said, lifting me back to my feet. "Not like this."

Before I could argue, he threaded his hands through my hair and brought our mouths together, pulling us both under the showerhead. His tongue tangled with mine while water cascaded over us, in the spaces between us. We were well past the point of pleasantries. This was an invasion. One I welcomed wholeheartedly.

Between the feeling of our warm, naked bodies rubbing together, the delicious aroma of his "clean woods" body wash, and the nimble fingers currently digging into my backside, my senses were beyond overwhelmed.

And then suddenly, we were moving. Rather than guide us out of the shower as I expected, he led us toward one of the bench seats, stopping when my legs met the edge. He lowered me down to the seat. A shiver raced over me when my bare ass met the cold tile.

"Too cold?"

"No."

Nothing was stopping me from swallowing this man's dick whole. Not my family, not my uterus, and definitely not an icy slab of marble.

I finally had a nonrefundable front row seat to Killian's cock. There was no going back now.

He reached down to push the wet strands of hair away from my face, tucking them behind my ears. His gentle touch and thoughtfulness, even during a bout of rough shower sex, never ceased to amaze me. Using his forefinger, he tilted my chin up until our eyes met.

"You ready for this, princess?"

I loved how vocal he was. That was something that set him apart from most of my previous sexual partners. But sometimes, actions spoke louder than words. So, to answer him, I fisted the base of his cock with one hand, used the other to peel back his foreskin, and swirled my tongue around the head, swallowing the precum already leaking from the tip.

His groan echoed through the stall. "That's a good girl."

Fuck. His words alone had me wiggling against the bench, desperate to make myself come. But this was his show, so instead, I circled the tip with my tongue a few more times before popping my mouth off him completely.

He fisted my hair. "Taste good?"

I summoned my inner most brat once more, angled my head back, and licked my lips.

"Tastes like mine."

"Mom, I don't think Dad needs another sweater."

"But it has owls on it."

Nellie and I both rolled our eyes. *This* was another Wheatley family Christmas tradition: Dad's hideous holiday sweaters. They didn't hold a candle to Angela Lansbury's. In fact, I'd venture that thanks to me and Killian's *Murder, She Wrote* binge, I'd never look at a sweater the same way again.

"I have an idea," I said. "What about instead of *another* sweater, you take Dad to see a show or spend the weekend at an Airbnb. That could be fun, right?"

"Hm, maybe." My mother was a woman hell bent on traditions. She'd sooner die than trade an immaculately wrapped sweater for a gift certificate, regardless of the impracticalities. "Oh! Look at that one."

Nellie waited until our mother walked over to peruse the sale rack before beginning her interrogation. "By the way, I couldn't help but notice you came back with wet hair and new clothes after your mad dash upstairs." She tilted her head to the side. "What was that about?"

I stared blankly. "I was suddenly feeling dirty."

"I bet you were." She smiled, waiting until I was almost out of ear shot before adding, "You ho ho ho."

We wandered over to the women's formal wear, where I proceeded to hold up dress after dress for her consideration. I needed to find *something* to wear to Killian's team holiday party.

"None of these are very you."

I threw up my hands. "I know that."

"Maybe you've got something at home already?"

"Maybe . . ."

"Or maybe your incredible sister needs to buy you some new wardrobe pieces for Christmas."

I scoffed. Janelle had incredible taste in clothing . . . that suited *her*. A straight-sized, athletic build body. She wouldn't know the first thing about dressing an apple-shaped size sixteen.

"Speaking of, I don't know what to give Killian for Christmas."

She wagged her brows. "Oh, I know what you could give him."

"Never mind. Forget I mentioned it."

She caught my sleeve before I could escape.

"Okay, okay. I'll be good. *Boring*, but good." She rounded the opposite side of the clothing rack. "What were you thinking?"

"I genuinely have no idea. What do you get the man who can buy himself anything?" I huffed. "Well, I did have one idea, but . . ."

"But what?"

"I don't know. It's kind of silly."

"Okay, well, now you have to tell me."

I gritted my teeth. "I thought I might make him a scarf."

"Make him . . ." Her eyes lit up. "You mean you're—"

"Just drawing, for now." I didn't want her to get too excited. Nellie was one of the few people who had supported my design dreams from the very beginning. In fact, we'd spent many hours creating looks for her Barbie dolls. "But yeah. In fact, I picked up some yarn yesterday. Is that crazy?"

"No, I love this!"

Yesterday was my first day back at the tearoom since my PCOS flare-up. To nobody's surprise, Bowie had been very understanding of my situation. The notoriety of Althea's Tearoom had exploded within the past year, largely thanks to Nora's rising star status on a hit TV show, so he had plenty of staff around to cover for the holidays.

When I finished my shift, I wandered into a yarn store a few doors down. Just to peruse, nothing more. Only perusing had turned into talking with the owner, talking had turned into comparing techniques, and before I knew it, I'd walked out with nearly a dozen skeins of yarn.

"I'm so proud of you, Leigh. You deserve this."

"Thanks." My cheeks warmed. "I don't know what came over me or why now, but I feel good about this."

"Maybe you just needed a fresh set of eyes." Nellie winked. "And hands." It was her exaggerated impression of a purring cat that set us both off.

Our mother found us a few minutes later, still trying to catch our breath while modeling overpriced sunglasses for each other.

"Leia, you will never guess what I found," she said, practically bouncing on her heels.

"Mom, don't worry about it." I'd already called off the search for a *Carol-oke* outfit. That didn't stop her from taking me by the wrist and dragging me back toward the formal section like a misbehaving toddler. "I'm sure I can scrounge something together from my closet."

"No, not that. Look."

She stopped us in front of an extravagant gown. A white gown. With a train. And one too many bows, and . . .

All at once, it clicked.

"Mom, this is a wedding dress."

"I know!" she cooed. "Isn't it perfect? Can't you imagine yourself wearing this as you walk down the aisle?"

"Mom, I don't want—"

"At our church."

"Mom."

"With a bouquet of pink freesias, and—"

"Mom!" I shouted, drawing the attention of nearly every last-minute holiday shopper in the store. I could practically hear it now:

"Attention Nordstrom shoppers, please direct your attention toward the bride-to-be about to go off on her mother in women's formal wear. That is all."

"Leighton Christina," Mom said, lowering her voice. *Oof, she middle-named me. That was never good.* "People are staring."

"People wouldn't be staring if you would just listen to me." I took a breath to calm myself. Killian was right. I might not be able to control my mom's thoughts and actions, but I could control the way I responded to them. "I don't want to look at wedding dresses right now," I said, evening out my voice. "I don't want to talk about my wedding right now or where I might want to have it. Not until I do my own research and discuss it first with my fiancé. Can you respect that?"

I leveled her with my best "I'm a grown ass woman who isn't afraid of what her parents think of her" stare. Even though I was (metaphorically) shitting myself.

Finally, after what felt like forever, she choked out, "Fine."

Huh. Would you look at that?

I didn't know who was more surprised, her or me. It might not have been the resounding, "Of course, sweetheart," I'd been hoping for, but it was a start.

Maybe this was a Christmas for new beginnings after all.

Killian

"It's in, it's in," Bowie chanted to himself, watching his ball roll closer to the edge of the green until, at last, it rolled off the edge.

The four of us—Bowie, Mr. Wheatley, Zia, and I—groaned in unison.

"Tough luck, mate." I slapped him on the back. "Don't quit your day job anytime soon."

"Fuck off," he replied. "I'd like to see you do better."

"You do remember I was a professional athlete, right?"

"This isn't the pitch, Kill."

"This isn't even golf," Mr. Wheatley added.

He was right. Despite the name, Top Golf wasn't exactly golf, but rather a combination of a driving range, sports bar, and arcade. A millennial man's—and one British lesbian's—wet dream come to life.

I was suddenly having flashbacks to the lifechanging blow job Leighton gave me in the shower this morning. *Blimey.* She'd sucked the life right out of me, along with my cum. The tightening in my pants was all the reminder I needed to save these thoughts for later, preferably when I wasn't standing three feet from her father.

Mr. Wheatley had been a last-minute addition to this outing. Zia, the avid golfer of the group, invited Bowie and I over a month ago, long before my arrangement with Leighton. When Leighton told me she'd be doing some holiday shopping with her mother and sister, I thought it best to invite Hank . . . er, Mr. Wheatley.

To say he was excited to go would be a bald-faced lie. In fact, he probably would have much preferred sitting back at the house, alone. But after some needling from Mrs. Wheatley, and a promise that he could order whatever he wanted from the bar and grill, he'd given in.

When we arrived two hours ago, we were assigned a second-floor corner bay, right by the bar, just as I requested. All in all, despite the nerves still pooling in my stomach (and wreaking havoc on my digestive system), we were getting along okay. He probably thought I had food poisoning since I'd run to the toilet four times already, but other than that, it was fine.

Maybe I'd win him over with my athletic abilities?

Fat chance. I'd already lost three hands.

We were currently in our second round of Top Shot, a game that challenged you to hit different-colored targets on the range. When my next turn rolled around, I set my feet, squared off from the ball, swung my club, and . . .

Bollocks.

"Sliced it," Mr. Wheatley said, as if I couldn't tell my shot was shit on my own.

"Oh, well done, *mate,*" Bowie taunted.

"Right, that's it." I set my club aside. "I'm going to grab another pint. Anybody else?"

Bowie and Zia both shook their heads. Mr. Wheatley, on the other hand, answered, "I'll go with you."

"Er, okay."

This was it; I could feel it. The moment I'd been desperately trying to avoid since Leighton had agreed to fake marry me. The dreaded one-on-one chat with my future father-in-law. Mr. Wheatley struck me as a more old-fashioned kind of bloke. After all, there was a reason Leighton had balked about her parents finding out about us living together, even before we were "living together." We still weren't living together, living together . . .

Bloody hell, I was confusing myself.

"So," he started as soon as we reached the bar. "What are you—"

"Mr. Wheatley," I said, cutting him off. My heart was already pounding at an unsteady rate. "I know you've just met me and well, we haven't had much time to get to know each other, but I just thought you should know I love your daughter. And unlike some people, I don't use that term lightly."

The room started to spin. *For fuck's sake, not now.*

"One second, please."

The last thing any of us needed was a repeat performance of last week's anxiety attack. Rather than race through the rest of my speech, I stopped. I had no doubt he was still watching me when I closed my eyes to focus on my breathing. I took my time. Anxiety wasn't exactly something you could turn on or off on a whim, but if I paid enough attention to the warning signs, I could stop the episode before it started.

I took a deep breath, and then another. I didn't know how long I sat there like that. It could've been a minute or maybe an hour. In any case, Mr. Wheatley's looming presence never waned. He didn't say anything, didn't interfere in any way. It was grounding in a way, to know that there was somebody there beside me, even when that somebody was Leighton's father.

I wasn't sure what to expect when I opened my eyes, but it wasn't Mr. Wheatley's hesitant smile.

"Mr. Wheatley, I'm sorry." I swallowed. "I have anxiety, and—"

"Finish your speech, son."

"Sorry?"

"You said that already." He took a sip of his beer. Apparently, I'd been out long enough for him to get a refill. "I don't think you were quite finished with your speech before. So, go ahead and finish it."

"Right." I hesitated under his glare. "Right. As I was saying, I don't throw 'love' around lightly, the word or the feeling. I've only ever loved three people. My mother, who I know would've loved your daughter. My oldest friend, whom you've just played a round of golf with. And your daughter, who I would be honored to spend the rest of my life with."

I swallowed the dry lump in my throat. *Damn, I should've saved this until after I ordered another pint.*

Just as I decided that another trip to the toilet might be in order, he said, "Okay."

That's it?

"Was there more?" *Bugger.* I didn't realize I'd asked my question aloud.

"Er, no. I suppose not."

He tipped his pint toward me before taking another sip. "I was only going to ask what you were drinking."

"What?"

"Before. I was only going to ask what you wanted to drink." *Great.* I'd inadvertently made myself look like a bigger prat than usual. "I already knew you were in love with her."

"You did?"

"It's pretty obvious, son." He clapped me on the shoulder. "For what it's worth, I think you're a fine choice for her. A perfect match, really."

That had me reeling. "Oh? And why is that?"

He set his glass down on the bar. "Leia has always carved her own path. She's not like the rest of us." *Here we go.* This was exactly what Leighton warned me about. "She never ceases to impress me."

Wait. What?

"Her mother, too. When it comes to Leighton, we live in a constant state of awe and panic." He twisted the ring around his finger. "She moved across the country to pursue her dream, she went to college, and she's lived on her own since she was eighteen. I barely finished high school. Hell, I can count on one hand the number of times I've been on an airplane."

Based off what Leighton had told me about her parents, that didn't exactly surprise me. What was surprising, however, was Mr. Wheatley's honesty. This man had spent the better part of December sitting sullenly in my favorite club chair. Come to think of it, this might've been the first time I heard him string together more than a couple words at once.

"Wanda and I want to be supportive. We do," he assured me, nodding his head for emphasis. "We just don't always know . . . how to."

I smiled with a newfound sense of understanding. "Have you told Leighton that?"

"Well, I . . . ," he trailed off, sheepishly scrubbing a hand over his grizzled jaw.

"Truly, Mr. Wheatley, I think that's all she's looking for. You don't have to understand her. Just support her." I shrugged.

"Killian," he said before downing the last of his pint. "You're going to be my son-in-law." My heart warmed the way he said it, so matter of fact. Now, if I could just convince his daughter. "I think it's well past time you called me Hank."

Chapter Eight

December 23rd

Leighton

I barely saw Killian over the next few days.

While he was finishing up the final few days of training before the team's winter break, I offered to cover a few morning shifts at Althea's. Seasonal staff or not, we were always bombarded with last-minute Christmas orders. Tea cakes, cookies, pies, you name it. Just yesterday, we hosted one of our holiday-centric "Leaves and Wreaths" events, where partygoers could enjoy traditional British tea service while also crafting holiday wreaths.

To nobody's surprise, the event was a huge success. Millennials, moms, and especially millennial moms loved "the experience." Something they could enjoy with their friends and talk about long after the event ended. The wreath was just an added take-home bonus.

Janelle had been nice enough to put up with Mom and Dad on her own the last few days. So, today, I was paying her back in kind the best way I could, by hooking the three of them up, free of charge, for today's Novel Tea Yours event. Althea's had partnered with The Ripped Bodice, a local bookstore devoted entirely to romance novels, for an afternoon of romance book recommendations (my mother's favorite) and tea pairings.

In addition to the winter dressing—dozens of paper snowflakes and twinkle lights, strung from end-to-end of the tearoom—each table had been decorated to match a particular romance trope or subgenre. Friends-to-lovers. Snowed in. Monster Fucking. That last one was new to me, but as a girlie who always rooted for Belle to get down with the Beast, *not* the prince, I understood.

I couldn't help but think about my and Killian's tropes. Opposites Attract. Fake Engagement. Only one bed. *That* was my favorite. Because no matter how little Killian and I had seen each other the last couple of days, we had seen plenty of one another in bed. I still hadn't felt him inside me though. And that was something I planned on remedying.

Tonight.

"Bowie, darling, what kind am I drinking now?" Mom asked from her seat. She, my dad, and Nellie had been seated at the forced proximity table. *Fitting.*

"That's the Cranberry of Convenience," he answered from the next table over.

"Oh! I just have to buy a bag for my book club. They're going to love it. Plus, it'll pair perfectly with our December book, *Winter Spice and Everything Nice.*"

Some other ladies at the table nodded. Dad, the sole male attendee aside from Bowie, sipped his tea quietly.

"I didn't know you were in a book club, Mom."

It didn't exactly surprise me. My mother was a collector of hobbies. As a stay-at-home mom, she'd always found ways to pack her days full of the three Cs: clubs, committees, and charities. Whether it was fundraising for the local library on wheels or co-chairing the Sidewalk Chalk Festival committee, she'd dabbled in a little bit of everything over the years. There wasn't a friend, neighbor, or stranger in Plain, Ohio who hadn't heard of Wanda Wheatley.

"We meet the last Friday of the month," she said, dodging eye contact.

I thought she was still reeling from our department store episode the other day. She wasn't upset, per se, and even if she was, my mother wouldn't dare to say so in public.

I didn't regret what I'd said, though. It was true . . . even if it was rooted in a lie. Someday, if I were to get married, what our wedding looked like, where it happened, and who was included would be entirely up to me and my spouse-to-be.

But, that didn't mean I wanted to exclude my family, especially my mother, who had no doubt been dreaming about Janelle's and my weddings since we were toddlers. Most of her friends' children were already onto their second and third children while we were pursuing law degrees and fucking around California. Even I could recognize that it must be difficult to reckon with.

For the first time, I was seeing things from a new perspective. Killian had suggested that my parents wanted to support me but didn't know how. That they didn't understand me.

Maybe, the same was true for them.

I had never understood their lifestyle. My goals had never aligned with theirs. I had never seen myself raising two kids in the suburbs or attending PTA meetings while my partner went off to work every day.

That wasn't *my* life. It never would be *my* life. But I could respect that choice and do my best to understand more about it, more about them.

Starting with something as simple as my mom's book club.

"What are you reading next month?"

"*The Rake's Guide to Murder and Matrimony.*" She studied me with suspicion. "Why?"

I lifted my shoulders. "Just curious, Mom."

"You never ask about my book club."

"Well, I just thought we could get to know each other better."

My mom stared back at me, utterly speechless.

Oh lord, I've done the impossible. I broke Wanda Wheatley.

Any clinking and clattering of plates at our table ceased immediately. The sisters from Salt Lake City hadn't known what they were in for when they sat down at our table. Afternoon tea *and* a show.

Like something out of a 90s sitcom, Bowie froze, teapot in midair. I snuck a peek at my sister, just in time to see her bury her face behind a plate of crumpets. Dad looked just as worried about this whole conversation.

"Isn't that what you want, Mom?" I pressed. "To know your daughter better?"

She blinked rapidly, giving an uncanny, unintentional impression of Bella Swan.

"Yes," she said, barely above a whisper. She cleared her throat, and repeated, "Yes."

"Good."

We sipped our tea in tandem. The subtle notes of cranberry and cloves soothed my suddenly dry mouth. Maybe it would be best to keep my mouth full of tea and scones.

Conversation around us continued. When I drained the last of my tea, I blew out my breath, unsure of where to go from here. Why did I have a habit of starting awkward, personal conversations in very public spaces?

"So . . ."

"So . . . ," my mom parroted.

I smiled. There was something comforting about the fact that we were *both* thoroughly uncomfortable.

"So, why don't we start our own book club in the new year?" Nellie offered.

"What?" I asked.

"You, me, and mom." Her attention bounced between the two of us. "We could take turns picking books and then talk about them on Zoom."

"While drinking tea?" I suggested.

"Sure!"

And then, in a move that surprised all of us, Dad covered Mom's hand with his own and said, "I think that sounds like fun. Don't you think, Wanda?"

Like Killian, my dad wasn't one for social gatherings. And not because he was anxious. No, he was simply a textbook case of introvert, with a side of "surly man over fifty" syndrome. The fact that he had come to tea with us at all was a true testament to the fact that he was trying.

The ball was in Mom's court now. A small part of me wanted her to say no. At least then, I would have a reason to continue avoiding her, blaming her. But selfish reasons aside, I wanted a relationship with my mother. With both of my parents. And I knew that that would require some changes. For all of us.

"That's a wonderful idea."

"Hm?" I asked. Had I heard her correctly?

"I think a book club with my daughters"—she paused, stretching one hand out to Nellie and the other to me—"would be lovely."

Relief washed over me. Nellie lifted her teacup in solidarity, bringing a smile to Mom's face. Dad caught my eye and winked, a surefire sign of approval. With one hand circling my teacup and the other laced through my mother's, I asked, "But can I make one request?"

"Sure, sweetheart."

"Can we not start with *The Rake's Guide to Winter Spice and Murder?*"

"Do we have to?" Killian whined.

I rolled my eyes. He sounded like a child being dragged away from his Saturday-morning cartoons.

"Killjoy, you're the coach. You can't *not* show up for your team's party."

He grumbled under his breath, but I couldn't make it out from inside the walk-in closet. I'd sequestered myself inside the massive closet—which was roughly double the size of my apartment bedroom—twenty minutes ago to finish getting ready for tonight's festivities.

My hair was curled. My makeup was done. I'd somehow shimmied into my hip-hugging (everything hugging) jumpsuit which left little to the imagination. As I finished securing the final few clasps of the corseted bodice, I ran the numbers.

Most people were well aware of "girl math." This was Los Angeles math.

The bar was twenty minutes away, so naturally, we needed thirty-five minutes, just in case. Parking would add ten minutes, plus an additional fifteen to walk back to the bar from our parking spot. Unless we did valet. That would save, basically, thirty minutes. Which meant if the event started at eight, and we wanted to arrive fashionably late by nine, we still had fifteen minutes before we *needed* to leave.

Simple math.

"So, what book did you decide on?"

I smiled to myself. When we got back from Althea's this afternoon, Killian had just finished a workout with Zia. I told him all about my breakthrough with my mom and we celebrated . . . with him eating me out in the shower. I tell you, if that man could do half the things with his dick that he could with his mouth and fingers, I was a goner for sure.

"Some dystopian thriller Nellie picked out."

"Sounds like something right up your mom's alley."

"You know it."

I fastened the final clasp before bending over—as far as I could in this outfit, which wasn't much—and tucking my boobs into place. I felt like *I* had just finished a workout. The fact that I had gotten myself into this getup was a Christmas miracle unto itself. I knew for a fact that it was over a decade old and handcrafted for a body one size smaller than mine, which was why when I found it, buried amongst my old fabrics and sketches, I spent the wee hours of the morning letting out the waist as much as possible.

This was one of my designs. Not crochet or knit, but rather a lace and linen creation from my first (and last) fashion show. Nothing else in my closet had felt right for the occasion, and there hadn't been any time to make something new. So, when I stumbled across this black number, I knew. It was this or bust. And, oh, the things it did for my bust . . .

A sudden knock at the closet door made me jump. "You alright in there?" Killian asked. "I'm hearing a lot of heavy breathing."

What will he think of my outfit? I wondered. *Well, no better time to find out than the present.*

I flung the closet door wide. "You try squeezing yourself into this without breathing heavily."

With the way Killian looked at me, I wondered if we would make it to the party after all. His eyes roved over my breasts, barely contained by the black lace and strategically placed flowers. Borderline indecent? Maybe in Ohio, but that didn't matter.

When he leaned against the doorframe, I couldn't help but do some admiring of my own. His well-defined arms flexed under his pinstripe dress shirt. He'd replaced his usual athletic shorts with a pair of custom-tailored slacks. A black leather belt finished the look, resting just above the erection I could already see pressing against his pants.

He grabbed me by the hips, slowly running his hands, fingertip by fingertip, over the exposed skin at my waist. I couldn't help the shiver or arousal that ran through me.

"You look good enough to eat, princess," he said, pressing his lips against my neck.

"Are you still hungry, killjoy?"

His eyes darkened. A knowing look spread across his face. "Always."

I groaned in need, which only made his smile grow.

"But I want to savor my meal, so it'll have to wait."

He laced his fingers through mine and guided me out of the bedroom. Once we were downstairs, I waited by the front door while he went to fetch our coats. He returned just in time to find me smoothing the linen over my ass.

My panty-line free ass.

"Are you wearing knickers?" he rumbled. "Please tell me you're wearing knickers."

"Sorry, killjoy." I turned toward the door, putting my ass on full display just to torture him. "Knickers don't go with this outfit."

This time, he was the one groaning.

Killian

The last two hours had gone a little something like this: twenty percent sharing cordial conversation with my team and staff, ten percent listening to Zia's girlfriend Blair butcher every song off the Mariah Carey Christmas album, and seventy percent envisioning Leighton's bare arse and cunt.

She had reduced me to a bumbling sod. One who could barely manage more than a sentence or two, all because the blood had drained from my brain to my cock. *My naughty girl.* These trousers were far too thin to conceal my erection, and there were already too many perverts in the world of sports, ergo I'd spent the evening hiding behind my fake fiancée, arm wrapped around her waist, holding her to me like some sort of security blanket.

There was no way she could miss the way my cock was pressing against her. At this point, I was so hard, I wouldn't be surprised if it left a dick-sized impression on her lower back.

The feeling's mutual, princess.

She had certainly left an impression on me. The memory of her in this outfit with that effervescent smile on her face would forever be tattooed on my brain. Maybe I'd tattoo it on my skin, too.

Best make things official before putting her on your body, mate.

"Are you okay?"

I angled my head down, my eyes finding hers immediately. Surprisingly, they were full of concern. "Fine, why?"

She scanned the room, ensuring we were out of earshot before answering, "You squeezed my hip. I thought maybe you might be overwhelmed or something?"

For fuck's sake, why did her genuine concern about my disorder make me want to bend her over and fuck her sideways?

I released my hold on her hip and twirled her to face me.

"I am overwhelmed." I tilted my hips, angling my cock so it would rub her in just the right place. Her eyes twinkled with lust. "Just not in the way you might be thinking."

"Maybe we should take care of that." She ran a hand down my jacket, tracing it down to my belt and then lower, to my . . .

Fuck.

"I'm feeling a bit overwhelmed myself."

I reached my limit when she squeezed me through my pants.

"Right, that's it."

Sadly, fate had other plans. We were flanked almost immediately by Cheyenne, her wife, Kayla, and Zia.

"Coach!" Cheyenne shouted, sloshing her glass of champagne.

"Fucking hell," I muttered under my breath. "Cheyenne, how are you?"

"Buzzed. But don't worry. The kids are with Kay's parents, so we've got the whole night to party!"

Kayla looked less than thrilled about spending her one child-free evening singing karaoke Christmas tracks. The feeling was mutual. I would much rather spend it in Leighton.

"Correction, we've got about one more hour before *this* one," Kayla said, gesturing toward my captain, "passes out from too much champagne and I catch up on *Only Murders in the Building*."

"Now, *that's* a party," Zia added.

"What did I miss? Where's the party?" This came from Blair, Zia's girlfriend. She'd temporarily set aside her microphone to wrap my assistant coach up in the biggest bear hug I'd ever seen.

Lord, people are getting too touchy. Time to go.

"You didn't miss a thing. We were just getting ready to call it a night."

"No!" Blair and Cheyenne protest in unison.

"You can't."

"You have to sing with us."

"Just one song."

"Please, coach."

They spoke over one another, with the same frenetic cadence, to the point where it was impossible to tell one from the other. So much for our smooth exit. How was I going to get out of this one? A party with my coworkers was one thing. Getting up on a stage to sing Christmas carols in front of all of them was another. There was no way.

"I'm so sorry, ladies," Leighton interjected, threading her fingers through mine. "Killian was just being nice to cover for me. I've got the worst cramps and—"

Suddenly, they were singing a different tune. And it wasn't Bing Crosby.

"Oh, say no more. You poor thing! Coach, take her home right away."

Reason #8: She'll do just about anything for the people she loves, even if it means making herself look bad.

Loves? If I could be so lucky . . .

Zia and I exchanged a knowing smile. I tipped my metaphorical hat and said goodnight while the rest of the women coddled Leighton. It took nearly ten minutes and one home remedy recommendation for soothing cramps before we made it outside.

"I have to say," I told her. "I wish men had some sort of fail-safe excuse to get out of things and bond over with strangers."

"What can I say? Misery loves company."

While we waited for the valet to bring the car around, I pulled her farther into the darkest corner of the building, crowding her against the bricks. My hands wrapped around her ass, dragging her body to mine at the same moment she pulled my mouth down to meet hers. We kissed for what felt like hours but couldn't have been more than a few minutes. I should know. I *had* kissed Leighton for hours.

I was the first to pull away, practically snarling. A feral animal ready to feast. "Are you going to put me out of *my* misery, princess?"

"Name the time and the place, killjoy."

"Now?"

Her tongue darted out, teasing my lips. "And the place?"

"I've got an idea."

"Killjoy, be honest," Leighton asked, breaking our lips apart. At this rate, we were going to need fast-acting ChapStick before the night was through. In my thirty-two years, I had never been so thoroughly kissed.

"Yeah?" I asked, rubbing my last two functioning brain cells together.

"How many girls have you fucked on the football field?"

I narrowed my brow, feigning outrage. "First of all, it's the pitch. Second, I'm a little offended you need to ask that."

When she asked me to pick a place outside the bar, a light bulb went off. What was the one place I felt more at home than home itself?

The pitch.

Plus, in order to do the things I wanted to do to her, we needed complete privacy.

"But," I said, dotting her nose with a kiss, "to answer your question, none." I trailed my mouth down her body, circling each nipple with my tongue, relishing the sigh that fell from her lips.

Fuck, her tits were perfect. Maybe someday, she'd let me fuck those, too.

I'd long since removed both our clothes. Now that she was naked in my arms, I could wholeheartedly admit that if getting into that jumpsuit was half as hard as removing it, she had every reason to be breathless.

"None?"

"None." I licked the crease of her belly. "Only." The curve of her hips. "You." And finally, her clit.

She squealed when I dove face-first into her pussy, throwing her legs wide to accommodate my shoulders.

"Goddamn," I murmured, to nobody but myself, before swiping first one finger, and then two through her pussy, gathering the wetness. She tried to move her hips, to take more, but I used the weight of my body to hold her still.

All in good time, princess.

"I want more," she moaned, her fists clenching in my hair, holding me to her clit. Drowning me in her pussy juices.

What a way to go.

When I finally gave her what she wanted, sliding both fingers deep inside her, she screamed.

This was exactly why I brought her here, why I paid Brian, the night security guard, five hundred bucks to take the rest of the night off. Out here, on centerfield at Sounders Stadium, there was only us. There was only this.

No family clamoring for attention.

No nagging boss or unruly customers.

Just the sweet smell of freshly cut grass and Leighton's scalding hot pussy clenching around my fingers.

"Killian." She tugged on my hair again, this time pulling my mouth off her entirely. "Please. I need you inside me."

I could spend the rest of my life on my knees eating her pussy, but I wasn't about to argue. Not when she was begging for my dick. When I reached for the condom in my wallet, she stopped me, placing her hand over mine.

"I'm on the pill," she said, the heat of her words searing my skin. "And there hasn't been anybody in over a year."

I swallowed. "You sure?"

"I trust you."

I didn't tell her how much that meant to me, that for every day of the year I'd known her, I had been waiting, earnestly, to win her trust. I didn't tell her that it had been nearly two years since another woman had touched my dick, four since it had actually been inside somebody. None of that mattered.

Nothing before her mattered. Only what came next.

Our eyes locked. I leaned over her, blanketing her body until there was no space left between us, lined my dick up to her pussy, and pressed home. I buried myself inside her, stretching her farther than I had before with my fingers or her vibrator. I pushed farther still, until my hips met hers and there was nowhere left to go.

"Fuck," she groaned, fisting my hair. "God, it's so much."

I knew exactly what she meant. This was so much more than sex. So much more than a physical connection.

"Too much?" I asked.

"No." She wiggled her hips. "I'm just . . . full."

"Not quite." It was a lie. She was already fucking full. But I was a greedy bastard, and I wanted more. So, I breathed through the exquisite torture and pushed her leg back, sliding it up and up until it draped over my shoulder. The new angle allowed me to press deeper still, until the head of my cock nudged the spot I knew would drive her crazy.

"Oh my god!" she screeched.

"Hang on, princess."

I held off long enough for her to wrap her hands around my shoulders, digging her nails into my skin. Then, I unleashed what had been building for months. No, a year.

I slammed into her. Over and over.

It was rough and needy. I was overcome with sensations and for the first time in forever, I welcomed them: Leighton's ragged breath warming my chest, my balls slapping against her ass every time I slammed deep, the biting pierce of her nails, digging into my flesh until I knew they'd leave a mark, the street noise somewhere in the distance. None of it scared me. On the contrary, I welcomed it, letting the chaos wash over me.

"Holy shit, killjoy!" Leighton cried when a particularly deep thrust had me rubbing against her G-spot. It wouldn't be long now. I flicked my thumb over her clit, eliciting another gasp.

"Say my name," I growled against her neck while my thumb continued its assault on her clit.

"Killian."

She whimpered when I pulled my hand away, then wailed when I brought it back down, this time slapping her clit.

"Yes?" I asked. I was all for testing her limits, but the last thing I wanted to do was hurt her.

"Yes!"

"Again, princess?"

"Killian. Yes, Killian." She was practically chanting my name, like a skipping record stuck in a loop. It was the best fucking song I'd ever heard.

I plunged into her over and over, slapping her clit each time I pulled out then massaging the sting away with every thrust back inside her. This give and take would be my undoing, but not before I felt her lose control.

Her breath was growing more ragged by the second. "I'm gonna . . . *Fuck,* don't stop."

"Come for me, princess." I pulled my head back, just far enough to look her in the eyes while I delivered one final slap to her pussy. "Come for me, *Leighton.*"

It was the sound of her name leaving my lips that sent her soaring into oblivion. And I wasn't far behind her.

I couldn't think. I couldn't breathe. Only feel.

And the feeling of her pussy milking my bare cock was too much to withstand. I was skyrocketing through space, already halfway to cloud nine, and it only took a few more thrusts to get me there. I didn't care where I was going, so long as Leighton was by my side. Or underneath me. Or on top of me.

As I groaned out my release against her neck and she combed her fingers through my hair, I hoped wherever we were, we never came back down.

Chapter Nine

December 24th

Leighton

It had been a long time since I stayed out until six a.m. Even longer since I had an all-night fuck fest.

And I had zero regrets.

After a second round on the pitch—not field—and a third round in Killian's office, we'd taken advantage of the Sounders' locker room showers to wash off the grass and . . . fluids.

And then, in a surprising twist because as I had learned over the last few weeks that this man was so much more than I expected, he just held me. Caressing every inch of my body with his hands and lips. Telling me how beautiful I was, how much he loved my lips, my neck, my butt dimples. Cherishing me. Until the shower spray ran cold.

When I woke up at nine, it was to the feeling of Killian's thick arms wrapped around me and a delicious ache between my thighs. When I woke up again three hours later, the space beside me was cool to the touch. As much as I wanted to stay where I was and soak up Killian's fragrant, earthy musk, there was still too much to do.

It was Christmas Eve and as Wheatley tradition dictated, it was time to bake the pastry wreaths. Christmas Eve was for baking; Christmas Day was for eating. Considering the time, I had no doubt that I was already in store for an earful from my mother. And a few snide remarks from Janelle, who had just been gearing up for her run when Killian and I got in this morning. *Busted.*

After I got dressed and used a few extra globs of concealer to cover up the beard burn on my neck, I put on my coziest slippers and trotted down the stairs. The sweet aroma of almond-y and yeasty goodness hit me before I reached the final step.

Along with a few familiar voices.

"Like this?" Killian asked, his deep voice tinged with wonder.

"That's perfect, sweetie. Now, the next thing you'll want to do is cut the rope in half longwise." After a beat, my mother added, "Do you want me to show you first?"

I pictured him nodding.

Instead of rounding the corner to the kitchen, I kept my body hidden behind the wall, leaning forward just enough to peek around the edge and see my mother demonstrating the proper knife techniques on the marble island. Killian observed every movement, thoroughly enraptured.

"Your turn." She handed the knife over and monitored his cuts. "That's good. Don't be afraid to use a bit more flour if things start to get sticky."

"Right." I admired his concentration. Baking was a skill both Nellie and I had never mastered, much to our mother's dismay. Well, at least Mom had Killian now.

Wait. That wasn't what I meant. I couldn't . . . We couldn't . . .

Oh, who was I kidding? This whole thing—moving in with Killian, our fake engagement, and my very real feelings for him—had been a sinking ship from the very beginning. I was barely treading water as it was. But I only had to keep my head above water for a few more days, right? Then, it would all go away.

That's what you wanted, right?

As much as I hated to admit it, this was a conversation that needed to be had with all parties involved. Internal monologuing was no way to solve my problems.

"Great work, Killian." Mom's praise was all it took to shake me out of my intrusive thoughts. "See, it looks just like mine."

The beam of joy that colored Killian's face was—to quote one of my dad's favorite movies—the "stuff that dreams are made of." They set the braided dough aside to rest while they worked on the fillings.

"Now, I don't know if you prefer nuts or fruit, but my grandmother's chocolate coconut filling is to die for. And it goes with just about anything."

Oh no. Coconut.

"Actually, Wanda," Killian hesitated. "I'm allergic to coconut."

"Oh."

"It's okay!" he assured her. "I just won't have any wreath. I don't want to interfere in your family's traditions."

The knot already forming in my chest tightened with his words. *This man.* Was there anything he wasn't willing to do to make me or my family happy?

"Sweetheart, that's terrible."

"I know." Killian rubbed the back of his neck, one of his nervous ticks. "I was really looking forward to trying them."

"No, I meant it's terrible that you think we wouldn't change that for you." She took his flour-covered hands in hers. "You're part of this family, too."

I felt my soul drain from my body, puddling on the floor beneath me. I might have melted into the floor entirely if the wall hadn't been holding me up.

"Besides," Mom continued, "I think it's about time we start some new family traditions."

"Er, okay," Killian stammered.

"So, what sorts of things did you and your mom do for Christmas?"

I slid to the ground, half-musing, half-listening as my mother and my fake fiancé discussed the ghosts of their Christmases past. This was the woman who had instilled in my sister and me from a very early age that family traditions were not to be messed with. That they were part of our "Wheatley legacy," one of the few things to pass from generation to generation.

And just like that, she changed her mind. Changed her entire belief system. Because of one smooth-talking Brit with a man bun and his coconut intolerance.

I thought that only happened in Hallmark movies.

When I finally regained my footing, I sidled up to the island.

"Well, there she is," my mom greeted. "Sleeping Beauty."

"Princess," Killian growled. One side of his mouth tipped up in a cocky grin, making my ears burn. I resisted the urge to smack that grin right off his face. I'd much prefer he slap my clit a few more times. Or maybe my ass.

"Are you okay, sweetie?" Mom asked, genuinely concerned. "You're looking a little pink."

Killian laughed and then covered it up with a cough.

"Fine," I told her. "It must just be a little warm in here. Everything looks great."

"Thank you!"

"Where are Dad and Nellie?"

Mom flurried through the kitchen without breaking stride, like she'd been baking in it her entire life. "They had to pick up a few things for dinner, plus some extra cranberries and cinnamon sticks. Killian and I decided to make a few extra wreaths for the neighbors."

I shifted my eyes between the two of them. "Oh, really?"

A small smile pulled at the corner of my lips when I noticed the splotch of flour on Killian's Henley. And another on his joggers. I liked him messy.

"Well," he started, looking up bashfully from the dough in his hands. "They loved your mum's cookies so it just made sense."

And even though my vagina was exhausted, well-used from the night before (and this morning, too), I nearly orgasmed on the spot when he smacked the ball of dough to the counter. A quick glance at his face told me he knew exactly what he was doing to me.

"Um," I croaked, pausing to clear my throat. "Do you mind if I do some present wrapping while you bake? I want to get it all done before dinner."

"Sure, sweetie."

"Need any help?" Killian asked.

"No." I leaned up on my toes to kiss his mouth. "You keep doing what you're doing."

His eyes, full of fire and promise, followed me back to the stairs. I took great pleasure in knowing that when I leaned over the banister for one last glimpse of him, he was still watching.

For the next few hours, I tuned out the sounds and smells from downstairs, turned up my favorite Hozier playlist—organized by tone, from "fucking in the forest" to "decomposing in the woods"—and knit.

The clock was winding down to Christmas and Killian's gift was nowhere near finished. Mostly because, as per usual, I had bitten off more than I could chew.

Knitting him a scarf hadn't felt good enough—not with everything he had done for me—so naturally, I decided he needed a hat as well.

And some mittens.

Or maybe they were one-toed socks? I couldn't quite tell yet.

It didn't help that I was out of practice either. A row that should've taken me twenty or so minutes to complete had taken double that. Even with my chunkiest knitting needles. But despite my frustrations, I was feeling more at ease than I had in months.

Well taken care of. Well fucked. Well loved.

Maybe?

We didn't need to dwell on the verbiage. I wasn't looking for a specific label for my and Killian's relationship. But there were a couple of things I needed to ask him, sooner rather than later.

I heard a knock on the bedroom door, followed by a tentative, "Leighton?"

"One second."

I hid the in-progress hat under Killian's pillow and tossed the rest of the yarn across the bed. I hoped he wasn't planning a pre-Christmas Eve dinner nap. Our bedroom looked like a war zone.

"Okay, come in."

He pushed the door ajar, poking his head through the opening. I cleared a seat for him on the bed next to me and gestured him over.

"I brought you some cocoa." He handed me the mug in his hand, steam wafting off the top. The warmth radiated up my arm and straight to my heart. "I didn't know if you preferred marshmallow or whipped cream, so there's a little bit of both."

"It's perfect. Thank you."

His eyes roamed our yarn-covered bed. "This doesn't look like present wrapping."

"I'll get to that eventually," I told him. I carefully set the hot chocolate aside and straddled his lap. "As soon as I finish your present."

His eyes widened. "*My* present?"

"Mm-hm." I threaded my hands around his shoulders, playing with the baby hairs at the base of his neck. He wound his arms around my back, resting them at the base of spine.

"You didn't have to get me anything."

"I know, but I wanted to." I leaned forward to nip his lips. "So, deal with it."

His fingers dipped lower, clenching on my ass. "You're asking for it, princess," he warned.

"Now, we both know I'm bad at asking for things." I ran my thumb over his full lower lip, averting my gaze.

"What is it?" he asked, sensing the change in my mood.

"I . . . I think I want to tell my parents." I swallowed. "About us."

"Tonight?"

I nodded.

"If that's what you want," he said with zero hesitation.

"It is."

"Okay." He smiled against my lips. I couldn't resist planting a frantic kiss on him, one that would hopefully hold him over for the next few days. Because as much as I wanted to drag us both back to bed—or the shower, or his office—and spend the rest of the year riding his face, my pussy needed to rest. Not to mention the fact that my family only had a few days left in town, and that meant we were going to be busy.

I knew that when we pulled our lips apart and he stared into my eyes, he saw the moisture gathering there. "Thank you," I whispered.

"Anything."

I climbed off his lap, and he left me to finish up my project. When he reached the doorway, he paused. "By the way, this doesn't change anything."

I stared at him, puzzled.

"Between us," he clarified. "No disrespect to your parents, but I don't give a fuck what they think about us. I waited a year for you. I'm not letting you go now."

He winked.

Little did he know that he had just answered my other question.

Killian

Dinner with Leighton's family didn't go exactly as planned.

Apparently, somewhere along the way to the grocery store, Hank had taken a right on Santa Monica Blvd, veered left onto Abbot Kinney, and run straight into the twilight zone.

Because when he and Janelle returned with dinner supplies, it wasn't the turkey and mashed potatoes they had discussed the day prior, the go-to Christmas Eve meal for the Wheatley family. Instead, his reusable grocery bags were packed full of sourdough loaves, sausages and several familiar blue cans.

"Wha—" I stopped, my eyes nearly popping out of my skull. "Sausage and beans?"

"That's right," Hank said, squeezing a very cheerful Wanda to his side. Had they planned this?

"We want this to be *your* Christmas, too, sweetie." Wanda rubbed my arm. "There's nothing like a taste of home, don't you think?"

When I came downstairs this morning, I hadn't intended to help with the Christmas wreaths. Truly, I just wanted a cup of coffee. But then, we got to baking and reminiscing, and before I knew it, I was spilling my guts to Wanda Wheatley.

I told her about my Christmases with Mum while Leighton slept off her sex-induced coma in our bed. I told her about how we would get all dressed up, like we were hosting Her Majesty, only to cook sausages and beans over a fire. It was all we could afford most years. I didn't complain. I told her about the age-old British tradition of Christmas crackers (the kind you pop, not eat) and paper crowns. And, most notably, I told her that I would trade the finest meal in all of England for one more campfire with my mum.

Sausages, beans, and toast. Just like the old days.

And now here I was, surrounded by the Wheatley clan, clinging to a seventy-nine cent can of beans like it was a priceless artifact. *Isn't it?*

I could feel my heart rate accelerating, approaching dangerous territory. That was the fickle thing about anxiety. It didn't discriminate between positive and negative emotions. Being overwhelmed was being overwhelmed, regardless of where you were and who you were with.

A cool palm slid into mine. "Want to take a walk, killjoy?" Leighton whispered against my neck.

I pivoted to face her. Her eyes skimmed over my face, not a trace of fear in them, but rather concern. She used a thumb to brush away my unshed tears.

For fuck's sake, where had that come from?

"No," I mumbled. "I'm okay."

With one hand still clutching the can of beans and the other clinging to Leighton's, I turned back to Hank and Wanda. I tried to find the proper words to express my appreciation, but all I could come up with was, "Thank you for this."

Straightforward, to the point. It would have to do.

"I've got some firewood in the car," Hank said. "Let's get that fire pit going."

"After you, sir."

I followed Hank toward the front door, pausing to turn back to Leighton and mouth, *Thank you.*

Anything, she mouthed back.

We waited until after dinner to break the news to Hank and Wanda. Because what kind of monster comes clean to their in-laws on an empty stomach? I don't know what Leighton had been expecting when we told them—shock, tears, maybe even an argument—but thankfully, they took it with grace.

And a few dozen questions.

"So, you weren't engaged when you invited us to stay?" Wanda asked, confused. We'd been at this interrogation for nearly twenty minutes.

"No," Leighton answered, her hand wrapped in mine. She had been my rock, my emotional lifeline several times already. It was my turn to be the grounded one.

"But you are now?"

"No!"

"But you are dating?"

Leighton looked at me for confirmation before saying, "Yes."

The four of us were still sitting around the fire pit. Janelle had snuck off to field another dodgy phone call. According to Leighton, she was waiting for the results of her bar exam, but that didn't explain why I'd seen her sneaking out in the wee hours more than once in the last few days.

"Now that you're together, do you still plan on moving out?"

Wanda didn't pull any punches, but it was Leighton's hesitation that stopped me cold. In all fairness, we hadn't discussed the future of our living situation just yet, but I thought I had made my feelings for her clear. Apparently not.

"I don't want her to," I said.

Wanda smiled, satisfied with my answer.

"Was everything we talked about true?" Hank asked.

I tried not to smile when I noticed the adorable crease forming between Leighton's brows. I hadn't told her about my episode at Top Golf. Or the conversation with her father that had followed. But Hank deserved an answer, so I figured this was as good a time as any.

"Yes, sir." I didn't bother running scenarios because as far as I could tell, there was only one play left in the game. "Nothing's changed. I love your daughter very much."

Nobody spoke after that. We were suddenly surrounded by complete silence, save for the sounds of crashing waves in the distance and the crackling fire. In hindsight, it might not have been the best moment to declare my love. For the first time. In front of her parents. Then again, timing had never been my strongest suit. If it had, I might have told her how I felt a year ago.

"You're not going to move back to England, are you?" Wanda screeched, shocking the piss out of all of us.

"Mom, what?"

"She already moved across the country," Wanda wailed, shifting her eyes to me. "I don't think I could stand it if she moved to another continent."

"Oh, Mom."

Leighton moved to her mother, cradling her head against her shoulder the way a parent might with their screaming child. Only this time, it was the child comforting her parent. As Leighton soothed her mother, I turned back to Hank.

"No," I said, fielding Wanda's question. "I don't plan on moving back to England anytime soon." I looked back at the woman who held my heart. Her eyes met mine from above her mother's head. "This is home."

Hank nodded, having heard everything he needed to hear. The evening wound down fairly quickly after that. Nothing soured the mood quite like a crying mother.

So much for leaving milk and biscuits out for Santa.

I put out the fire while Hank dried his wife's eyes and after that, we all turned in. But it wasn't time for bed just yet. This conversation with Leighton was far from finished.

Even as we changed into our pajamas, I could feel the waves of tension radiating from her body.

"You want me to keep living here?" she finally asked, breaking the terse silence.

"Why does that surprise you?"

"Oh, I don't know. Probably because you never mentioned it."

"Well, I'm mentioning it now." I sat down on the bed, leaning back on my elbows to watch her pace. This angle did amazing things for her tits. "You don't want to stay with me?"

"I didn't say that."

"So, you do want to stay?" I teased.

She rolled her eyes. "I didn't say that either." To say she was irritated would be an understatement.

"Would it make you feel better to have your own room again?"

That gave her pause.

"That would be . . . okay?"

"Of course," I said, taking her hand in mine. "I know we sort of went about this in all the wrong ways, but we can take things as slow as you like. Rewind, even, if you want."

She heaved a sigh of relief.

"That doesn't mean I'm not going to try and convince you to share my bed every night." She let out a little snort that sent a jolt of pleasure down my body, all the way to my toes. "I've grown very fond of you there."

"What about the other thing?"

I lifted my brows, feigning ignorance. "What other thing?"

"You *know*."

"I *know* what?"

"Killian . . ."

"Leighton . . ."

"You said that you love me!" she blurted out.

I tried (and failed) to bite back my smile. The horrified look on her face made it impossible not to laugh. She playfully shoved me away, or tried to at least. Instead, I gathered her into my arms, pulling her down on top of me on the bed. My cock twitched when she swiveled her hips. The blasted fucker had been in a semi-hard state all day.

When she finally settled in my lap, I cupped her face and relayed the message my heart had been playing, over and over, for nearly a year.

"Because I do," I said, speaking slowly and with conviction. If she wanted, nay, needed to know how I felt about her, I was going to make it crystal clear. "I love you, Leighton. And I don't expect you to say it back right this second, but I'll say it again, every day until you believe me. And then, I'll tell you twice a day because I want it to be the first thing you hear when you wake up in the morning and the last thing before you go to sleep in my arms."

She didn't shy away from my penetrating gaze. But she did, much to my horror, start to sob.

Well done, you knob.

I kissed a fallen tear from her cheek. "Shit, princess. Do you hate me?"

"Killjoy," she said, tugging my head back until she could see my eyes. "You make it impossible to hate you."

After that, there was nothing left to say.

Not with words anyway. We let our tongues do the talking.

I snaked a hand inside her leggings, tracing the elastic band of her panties back-and-forth before finally dipping inside. She was already slick for me. Her lower body nearly lurched off my lap when I slid my finger lower, into her heat.

"I hate to break it to you," she said between kisses, "but my pussy is swollen as hell. There's no way you're putting anything inside there tonight."

I smiled wickedly.

"Who said anything about your pussy?" I asked. At the same time, I trailed my fingers from her pussy back toward her ass, testing her puckered entrance.

Her cheeks lit up like a goddamn Christmas tree.

Chapter Ten

Christmas Day

Leighton

"Is he . . . ?" Nellie trailed off, dumbstruck by the view. I couldn't blame her.

"Yup," I said proudly, popping the "p."

And why shouldn't I be proud? I had a super sexy boyfriend.

Sigh. Boyfriend.

It was official. Killian and I had had *the* talk last night in bed. Right after he finished eating my ass while watching *Murder, She Wrote.* That had been a first. The memory alone made my entire body tingle.

If someone had asked a month ago where I would be Christmas morning, I never could've imagined this: my nose pressed to a wall of windows, sipping coffee from a machine with a name I couldn't pronounce, ogling my fake fiancé turned real boyfriend alongside my baby sister.

Killian was back to swimming in the buff. He had probably figured he could get his workout in well before the rest of the house woke up. That might've been true on any other day of the year, but not on Christmas morning.

Christmas Day with the Wheatleys was an Olympic sport.

One that began promptly at seven a.m. and ran according to schedule until the final bite of my mother's spice cake.

Which was why the Christmas wreaths were already warming in the oven and Nellie and I were onto our second cups of coffee.

"He's got good—" I lifted my brows, daring her to finish the sentence. "Form."

"Mm-hm." If she only knew.

When her phone lit up, a sudden thought crossed my mind.

"By the way, where did you disappear to last night?"

"Um," she said, floundering. Come to think of it, Nellie had been uncharacteristically quiet lately. And missing in action from more than a couple family dinners.

"What's going on? Is it about the bar? Did you pass?"

"Shh!"

I didn't know why she was being so secretive. Aside from Killian, who was balls deep in his butterfly stroke, there was nobody else around to hear us.

Dad had ducked out for his annual Christmas cigarette that all of us pretended we didn't know about. Mom was still upstairs getting dressed and probably putting a full face of makeup on. She never went anywhere where people were likely to see her, or take photos of her, without her "face" on. Her words, not mine.

"Yes, I passed."

"Congratulations!" I threw my arms around her, narrowly dodging her cup of coffee.

"Thank you, but . . ." She chewed on her bottom lip. "There's more."

"What is it?"

She turned away from the window. *Damn*. Whatever it was, it had to be bad if she was willing to walk away from spying on my smokeshow of a boyfriend.

"I was offered a job," she said after getting comfortable on the couch.

I blinked. "You're joking? Already?" I couldn't help but feel like there was more to the story. "Isn't that a good thing?"

"The job is in Beverly Hills."

Huh. That was puzzling. From what limited knowledge I had on the subject—most of which I had learned from watching *Legally Blonde* and late-night reruns of *Boston Legal*—every state required you to take a separate bar exam. Which would mean . . .

"I never took the Ohio bar," she said, drawing her shoulders up to her ears. "But I *did* take it for California, New York, and Massachusetts."

"Oh. My. God." Our parents were going to shit a brick.

"Believe me, I know."

"You have to tell Mom and Dad."

"I will." She paused to sip her coffee. "But not today. I'd say they've endured enough truth bombs for one Christmas, don't you think?"

We clinked our mugs together in solidarity and then sat back in silence, taking in the scene of the roaring fire, the stockings, overflowing with books, knick-knacks, and, presumably, a brand-new Christmas mouse, and, of course, the tree. It was dressed top to bottom in white lights, silver and gold ornaments, and had a Minnie Mouse angel on top.

It was all so familiar, and yet completely brand new. The perfect combination of Christmas past, present, and future.

Well, humbug.

"So, what do you think?" Nellie asked, clinking her flawlessly manicured fingers against her mug. "Think you could stand having your sister around a little more often?"

I smiled from behind my coffee mug. "I think I'll manage."

Just then, the sliding glass door opened. I felt his presence, even before he laid his hands on my shoulders.

"Morning. Merry Christmas, Janelle."

"Merry Christmas," Nellie echoed.

I tilted my head back to see him. Bare ass gliding through the water Killian was a sight to behold, but he was no match for "wet hair, don't care" tattooed Killian.

He grinned when I reached up, twirling a loose lock of hair between my fingers.

"Merry Christmas, princess."

"Merry Christmas, killjoy."

I dragged his mouth down to meet mine, fulfilling every millennial woman's dream of recreating the upside-down *Spider-Man* kiss. The ends of his wet hair dragged and dripped across my face.

"Ugh." I recoiled. "You got me all wet."

"I certainly hope so," he whispered against my forehead. "I'm going to hop in the shower. Is there a plan for today?"

My sister and I exchanged a pointed look and then burst into laughter. His eyes met mine, full of worry and concern. For us, probably, when really, the only person he needed to worry about was himself.

"Oh, Killian," Nellie said, drying a tear from the corner of her eye. "You have no idea what you're in for."

"C'mon, Hank, shake your ass!

There was something I could've gone my entire life without hearing my mother say.

But as we all knew, and as Killian was apt to realize (whether he wanted to or not), anything was possible during the Wheatley Winter Games. The annual minute-to-win-it style tournament brought the best (and the worst) out in each of us.

Nellie's cup stacking skills, that she'd honed during one too many games of beer pong in grad school, was legendary. Lawyers went hard.

Dad had laser-focused precision. Who knew he had a talent for balancing ornaments on an empty paper towel tube?

And of course, Mom flaunted her over-the-top, competitive nature.

"Harder, Hank! Harder!"

I buried my face behind a pillow while my mom coached Dad on his twerking skills, or lack thereof. I could only imagine what Killian must be thinking. Nellie and I had done our best to prepare him for today's activities, but there were some things you couldn't explain, no matter how well you tried.

Jingle Your Junk (in the Trunk) was one of them.

A game that involved trying to bounce jingle bells out of the empty tissue box strapped around your hips. Hence, the vigorous hip-thrusting and ass-bouncing. Where did Mom come up with this?

I could only imagine what Killian must be thinking. I snuck a peek at him from behind the pillow clutched to my face. Much to my surprise, he was riveted, eyes bouncing back and forth between my dad and the stopwatch in his hand. My cheeks heated when he turned his head and caught me staring, but that was nothing compared to the warmth in my heart.

Killian had embraced my family wholeheartedly—in all their loud, meddlesome, ass-shaking glory—and they had welcomed him into the fold. What more could a girl ask for?

"Time," Killian called out, while also marking it down on the clipboard. "Two minutes, forty-nine seconds. That makes Nellie the champion with . . . thirty-two seconds."

Like I said, lawyers knew how to party.

"Read it and weep, Wanda," Nellie taunted. "These hips don't lie."

Nellie continued bouncing her butt for all to see, while my dad tried to catch his breath.

Killian leaned over and whispered, "Your dad might need a water break."

"The rest of us might need another mulled wine break. I'll get that started."

It was going to take a lot of liquor to make it through the day. We'd already been at this for hours and had barely made a dent in Mom's line-up of games. *We Wish You a Merry Fishmas, Holiday Nutstacker, The Toasts of Christmas Past.* Coffee had gotten us through the first few games, but alcohol would be necessary for the rest.

At least the edible I took with breakfast had kicked in.

I stirred the hot wine and brandy simmering on the stove. The sweet fragrance of cinnamon and cloves flooded my senses. When a heavy set of arms wrapped around me, I tilted my head back, resting it against Killian's chest.

"Are you good?" I asked him. "I know this is . . . a lot." It was just the five of us, though Blair and Zia mentioned they might pop by later this evening. Bowie and Nora were also hoping to join us for a post-Christmas dinner drink.

He nodded. "Great, actually."

Relief washed over me. There was a sense of ease about him to-day that I hadn't noticed before. I couldn't help but think that our fake engagement had been an unnecessary burden holding him down. Now that we had come clean to my family, the weight had been lifted.

"I had forgotten what it was like," he mused.

"Hm?" I asked, shaking my head.

"A family Christmas."

He must have noticed my crestfallen expression because he kissed my forehead.

"Don't be sad, princess," he whispered, his lips lingering just above my brow. "It's a good thing, I promise. You might not think so, but you've given me an incredible gift."

For a moment, I stood there frozen, staring at him. The longing expression in his eyes was all the gift I needed.

"Janelle, you used the cotton balls to mop up your spilt wine. How are we supposed to do the snowball toss?!"

And just like that, the moment was over.

"An incredibly *loud* gift," Killian amended.

Maybe next Christmas, I'd give my mother the gift of good timing she so desperately needed.

Killian

"Oh wow, Wanda, it's a . . . jack-o-lantern mouse?" Nora asked, her voice nearing a pitch intended only for dogs.

Nora elbowed Bowie's side when he started to giggle. He did his best to cover it up with a well-timed cough. "It's very creative," he added.

"Thanks, Mom." Leighton held up her newly acquired Christmas mouse and pasted on her most convincing smile. "I love it."

Bowie and Nora had joined the festivities sometime between dinner and charades. Perfect timing if you asked me. I was *shite* at charades. Zia and Blair had also stopped by briefly, just long enough to exchange some homemade cookies for one of Wanda's pastry wreaths.

The day had been an endless stream of comings and goings, meeting neighbors I had barely exchanged more than a couple of pleasantries with before now, celebrating with old friends and new family, and drowning my sorrows—because I hadn't won a game all day—in mulled wine and baked treats. All in all, aside from my piss poor gameplay, it was the best Christmas I'd had in years.

"How come Leighton got a jack-o-lantern mouse and I got gynecologist mouse?" Nellie whined.

"It's supposed to be a judge."

"Then why is it holding a speculum?" Judging by the quirk of Nellie's lips, she was egging her mother on. *That* was the real gift.

"For heaven's sake, that's a gavel."

As mother and daughter bickered back and forth, my eyes scanned over the room, taking in the mess of discarded wrapping paper and decorative bows, the boxes of candles and cooking supplies that had long since been opened.

Bowie and Nora had cozied up on the opposite end of the sectional. It warmed my heart to see my best friend so deliriously happy. Just last year, we'd been celebrating Devin and Riley's Christmas nuptials. Something told me that by this time next year, I'd be dancing at his and Nora's wedding.

Hank was polishing off his third piece of spice cake, wearing the most ridiculous jumper I'd ever laid eyes on. He hadn't balked when his wife presented him with the knit mishmash of silver and gold woodland creatures. On the contrary, he'd thanked her profusely and donned the monstrosity for the rest of the evening.

He and Wanda had accepted my open invitation to the U.K. in lieu of a wrapped present under the tree. After a month of firsts, I was chuffed that I could give them one as well: the first stamp in their passports.

"Do you like your present?" Leighton asked. She cozied up to my side, adjusting the skirt of her dress so it kept all my favorite bits covered. It was my first time seeing her in a dress and *fuck*, I hoped it wouldn't be the last. Her ass and legs should come with a warning. Rated M for Mine.

"I love them," I told her honestly. I was still having a hard time figuring out when she had managed to carve out enough time to knit me a hat and scarf, both in the Sounders' team colors of black and red. A true testament to her talent, I supposed. "Especially the scarf. It gives me . . . lots of ideas."

Her eyes sparkled with something akin to desire.

"What sort of ideas?"

"Oh, you know." I wrapped the scarf around her. The action was innocent enough not to elicit any attention from her family or our friends. But they didn't know the filthy, depraved things I was imagining. "You. In this scarf. And nothing else."

"Hm, that could be arranged." She covered my hands with hers.

"Or," I continued, lowering my voice, "you tied to my bed."

She walked her fingers up my chest. "Maybe I want to tie *you* to the bed."

I couldn't contain my shit-eating grin. Or the erection straining against my boxer briefs.

As much as I wanted to hear more about her "tie me up, tie her down" fantasies, there was still one last gift that hadn't been handed out. One that didn't fit under the tree.

I stood and offered her my hand.

"Sorry," I said, loud enough to gain everybody's attention. "Do you mind if I steal Leighton away for a few minutes? I need to show her something upstairs."

They all waved me off and went back to their dessert and conversation.

Leighton questioned me the entire way up the stairs. When we reached the landing, I covered her eyes the rest of the way until we reached the final door at the end of the hall. Only then did I remove my hand.

Her eyes bounced between me and the closed door.

"You got me . . . your office?" she asked. "Oh, you shouldn't have!"

"Smart ass," I said, punctuating with a slap to her ass.

I reached around her, opening the door to what *had* been my office and what (I hoped) would now be her studio.

She gasped, first with surprise and then with realization.

On one side, a hydraulic standing desk big enough to accommodate all her sketching and sewing needs. The bookcase on the opposite end had been cleared off and, thanks to some help from Bowie and Janelle, stocked full of yarn. Shelf after shelf, there was skein after skein of wool, alpaca, even bamboo. A kaleidoscope of colors, organized according to the rainbow, per Bowie's demands.

Needles had been organized in vintage coffee tins, according to size. The same went for pencils, pens, and scissors. And though she couldn't see it, the closet was full of fabric bolts, in case she decided to venture beyond knits. But the pièce de résistance was the electric blue dress form in the corner. It had taken me two weeks and nearly forty phone calls, but I had finally tracked down a full-figured sewing mannequin.

"How did you—"

"I had some help."

She wandered around the room, sizing up every shelf, every tool. Running her fingers over the yarn, pinching it between her fingers.

I stood back, cataloguing the range of emotions on her face.

"What do you think?" I asked.

She sucked in a breath. "It's amazing." Her eyes met mine, glistening with unshed tears. "I can't believe you did this for me."

"Princess," I said, shaking my head. I wrapped an arm around her waist and dropped a kiss to the crown of her head.

Crown. Princess. Ha!

With a lopsided grin, I reminded her, "You should know by now that I'd do just about anything for you."

It was going on half past eleven when I felt her come up behind me in the kitchen.

"I hope you're not too tired for one more game," she whispered, her warm breath fanning my ear. Even though I was an athlete, I didn't know how many more nonsensical cup-stacking or biscuit-balancing games I could take. My eyes were already nearing half-mast.

"Pretty sure that was the last one. Your sister already passed out."

I nodded toward the couch. Janelle had indeed fallen asleep on the sofa—paper crown and all—halfway through "Christmas Ball," a game that involved using a gift-wrapped box as a fan to propel a holiday ornament across the floor.

"This is more of a two-person game."

That had me raising my brows. "Oh yeah?"

"Mm-hm." She handed me a can of whipped cream, still dripping with condensation from the fridge. When my eyes met hers, I recognized that devious glint that I had come to love so much. The one that turned her honey-brown eyes a richer shade of chocolate.

All of a sudden, I was wide awake.

"Time for bed," I announced, my voice cracking at the end. A nervous giggle tumbled out of her when I all but dragged her up the stairs to our bedroom.

As soon as the door closed behind us, I was on her. A torrential frenzy of hands, lips, and teeth.

My mouth tore at hers while I held her against the door with the weight of my body, my thick length digging into her belly. I pulled down the top of her dress, low enough to expose her puckered nipple and take it into my mouth.

"Tell me more about this game," I said around a mouthful of Leighton's tit.

"I'd rather show you."

I led her toward the bed then doubled back to the loo for a towel. I had a feeling this game might be messier than the rest.

She was waiting for me on the bed when I got back, lying on her stomach, kicking her feet back and forth behind her. I turned to the vanity to remove my cufflinks. Dressing up for Christmas dinner had been a gas, but I couldn't wait to get us both naked.

I watched her through the vanity mirror.

"You look good on my bed."

"I'd look better bent over it," she said, smiling cheekily. "Don't you think?"

And then she shocked the hell out of me by doing just that. She stood up, turned around, and bent over the bed, leaning forward until her elbows met the duvet, exposing the bare globes of her ass.

And the bejeweled butt plug tucked between them.

"God, I love you."

I tossed the towel aside, whipped cream and cufflinks forgotten as well, and nudged her legs farther apart. Her eyes narrowed when I opened the bedside drawer, and then lit up when I removed the tube of lube we'd cracked open last night.

"Is this what you want?" I said, smacking a hand across her exposed bottom.

She squeaked in surprise, jolting forward a few inches. I pulled her back, wedging my cock against the opening of her wet cunt. She rubbed herself against the seam of my trousers, no doubt leaving a wet mark. Her whimper turned into a moan when I smoothed a hand over her ass cheek, admiring the tint of red on her pale skin before smacking it once more.

She squirmed, subtly hinting that she wanted more. I was all too willing to give it to her, but first, she would need to ask for it.

"What do you want, princess?"

She wiggled against my dick. My arms banded tighter around her, holding her in place while I spanked her once more.

"Use your words, Leighton."

I rained kisses down her freshly spanked skin before circling back, peppering her ass, waist, and thighs with feather-soft kisses.

"What do you want?" I asked again.

Third time was the charm. She peered at me over her shoulder, smiling dangerously and cocking one eyebrow.

"I want you in my *arse.*"

Fuck, she's trying to kill me.

My shoulders vibrated with laughter, which set her off, too. Only Leighton could take me from wanting to bend her over and fuck her ass one minute to laughing mine off the next. Just another reason to add to my list.

"Alright, princess," I said, lifting my head when I finally regained my composure. "Let's test this scenario."

Epilogue

New Year's Eve

Leighton

"I can't believe you talked me into this."

I looped Killian's wrist through the scarf before wrapping it around the headboard. Once I was sure it was secure, I climbed over his bare chest to do the same to his other wrist.

"You asked me how I wanted to ring in the new year," I said, batting my eyes.

"I know, but—"

"Sounds like somebody might need to make 'being better at giving up control' one of their new year resolutions."

"That's not happening," he said with a pointed glare. "Besides, I don't believe in resolutions."

There were only hours left to go before the clock struck twelve. We'd arrived in Big Bear earlier today, just in time to beat the onslaught of snow. It was shaping up to be a very snowy New Year's Eve, but that didn't phase me one bit. Thanks to Bowie's generous gift, Killian and I had four uninterrupted days ahead of us in this cozy, A-frame cabin.

And I planned on taking advantage of every moment and every surface. Starting with the knotty pine—more like *naughty* pine—king-size bed.

Killian's hand tensed when I knotted his second wrist. He didn't like being out of control, in or out of the bedroom. But I knew the truth. He was only grumbling because he was butthurt that *I* was the one tying *him* up with his newly acquired Christmas scarf and not the other way around. The erection probing my ass was a pretty *big* indicator that he was still up for the task, so to speak.

"Do you need a safeword?" I asked, sliding down his chest, my pussy leaving a wet trail in its wake. He'd already made me come twice tonight, once while finger-fucking me on the couch and then again while riding his face.

It was his turn to be at *my* mercy for once.

He shook his head. "You'll stop if I ask you to. Just as I would for you."

Of that, I had no doubt. Killian was by far the most considerate lover I'd ever had, not that there were very many to compare him to. I was picky when it came to who I trusted with my body. Even pickier when it came to my heart. I wanted to give Killian everything.

He tugged at his bonds, but that only tightened them further.

"You good?" I asked, reaching behind me to stroke a hand down his cock, using his precum to lube him up.

"*Yes,*" he hissed.

"Too tight?"

I teased his tip at my entrance.

"No."

He groaned when I lowered myself onto him, gliding his length into me, all the way to the hilt.

"How about now?" And because exquisitely torturing us both was too tempting to resist, I squeezed around him, causing him to groan once more.

I looked down at where we were connected, marveling at the graphic way he stretched my pussy, my arousal coating him. It was better than any porn clip I'd ever seen. Maybe one day, I'd ask him to film us.

"Princess," he growled through clenched teeth. "You're fucking killing me."

I smiled at him through hooded eyes. "Well, we can't have that."

I lifted my hips, using my palms on his chest for leverage, before falling back down, taking him as deep as he could go.

I'd always had a love-hate relationship with being on top. On the one hand, I found it empowering. I loved being in control of the pace, of his pleasure and mine. It was a welcome contrast to the whirlwind of my everyday life. On the other hand, I was a pillow princess through and through. Scratch that. More like a rag doll, one who enjoyed getting tossed around.

I ground down on Killian again, rubbing my clit against his pelvis, which nearly had me seeing stars. My eyes raked over every inch of his defined chest, each swirl of ink that covered his arms and torso. It was a stark contrast to my pale, virgin skin.

A pained smile graced his lips as he watched me take his cock over and over.

"Fuck, look at you," he strained. "You're so fucking gorgeous, Leighton."

My breath hitched. *Gawd, I love it when he says my name.*

"Come up here. *Please*," Killian begged, pulling at his restraints. "Give me your tits."

I inched forward, dangling my breasts over his face like a sacrificial offering. He latched onto my left breast first, scraping his teeth across the nipple before lightly biting down. For a second, I lost my motion and plummeted back down onto his cock, causing us both to moan.

He took advantage of my lapse in control and switched to the other breast. This time, after biting down, he sucked. I felt the burst of pleasure-pain vibrate all the way to my throbbing clit.

"Fuck," I cried out, trying to regain rhythm. "The things you make me feel."

"Like what?" He licked the bead of sweat between my breasts.

I was at a loss for words. So instead, I kept riding him. My head tipped back of its own volition. I closed my eyes, soaking up the feeling of his bare cock grinding so perfectly on my G-spot. I was so close. There was no doubt in my mind that my pussy juices were dripping down his balls.

"What do I make you feel, princess? Safe?"

"Mm," was all I could manage.

"Worshiped?" He lifted his hips that time, thrusting up into me. *Bastard.*

"*Yes,*" I moaned.

"Loved?"

"Yes!" My inner muscles flexed around him.

"And do you love me?"

My eyes flew open. Killian had stopped moving. He just stared into my eyes, waiting for an answer to his question.

As promised, he had told me he loved me every day since Christmas. And every time he had told me, I had chickened out. I bared my soul to this man, shared my deepest wounds with him. Shared a bed with him. Shared my body—every inch of it—with him. And yet, there was one thing I hadn't given him yet.

"Yes," I breathed, barely above a whisper.

"Yes what?"

"Yes, I . . ." I licked my lips and looked him in the eyes. "I love you."

The energy in the room shifted. Before I could so much as blink, Killian—my boyfriend, my roommate, the man that I loved—seized up, freeing himself from the restraints.

"Wha—"

He flipped us over, nearly knocking the wind out of me when he landed on top, between my thighs.

"How did you—"

He leaned down, his lips seeking mine. He kissed me just as slowly as he was fucking me, with a newfound sense of reverence and devotion. This wasn't a race to the finish. No, this was another promise. An oath, as Taylor Swift would say.

When he pulled back, he took both of my hands in his and moved them over my head.

"You might want to hang on for this, princess."

He drove into me, punishing thrust after punishing thrust. My fingers grasped for the headboard, searching for purchase. When he drew my knee up, sinking inside me deeper than before, I screamed.

Forget the fireworks. Forget the noisemakers.

At the rate Killian was drilling into me, the entire neighborhood was likely to know my scream before the ball dropped tonight.

"That's right, princess," he said, whispering into my ear as he hammered into me, "Let me show you how much your man loves you."

Killian

Later, while Leighton used the restroom after we finished making love—because nobody wanted to start the new year with a UTI—I leaned over the bed, searching for my discarded trousers. When I found them, I drew a folded piece of paper and pen out of the left pocket. I'd been keeping both of them in there recently for moments just like this.

I quickly jotted down reason number one hundred.

Reason #100: She loves me.

"Did I tell you that I signed up for that Valentine's Day artisan market in Santa Monica?" she called out. There was no intimacy quite like conversing with your significant other while one of you was on the toilet.

"That's brilliant."

"I should have a decent amount of stock by then."

Rather than move out or quit her job at the tearoom, Leighton had decided to cut back on her work hours to focus on her designs. With a free place to stay—because there was no way in hell I was making her pay rent—and her new office space, there had never been a better time or opportunity for her to pursue her fashion dream. She still contributed to the household groceries and utilities, despite my best protests. But so long as she was happy and in my bed every night, I didn't mind.

"What's that?" Leighton asked, sneaking up behind me.

"Nothing." I clutched the paper to my chest.

"I saw my name at the top of it." She eyed me with suspicion. "Oh, god, are you writing me some cringey, romantic love letter."

"No."

"It's okay if you are. I promise, I won't be embarrassed."

"No."

"Okay, you're right. I *will* be embarrassed." She flopped down on the bed without a hint of self-consciousness. "But I promise, I'll pretend not to be embarrassed."

The real question was, would I be? Was it worth risking this final piece of my heart? She already had the rest of it.

Decision made, I rolled toward her until we were lying side by side, blissfully nude.

"Do you want to read it?" I offered her the paper, grateful that I hadn't sweat all over it. I was shaking like a leaf on the inside.

"I was just kidding, killjoy. You don't have to show me if you don't want to."

"I do."

Her gaze flickered over the paper with a hint of curiosity. She took it from my hands, balking when she saw the title. I'll admit, "Reasons Why I Love Leighton Wheatley" wasn't the most creative, a B+ at best. But the reasons that followed, all one hundred of them, were distinctly unique to the exceptional woman in front of me.

Her brow lifted when she read the first line, but then fell back into place when she read the next. And the next. And the next. She read the list from top to bottom, and then, for good measure, she read it in reverse. And that was how we spent the next few hours: counting the reasons I loved her while counting down to the new year.

When the clock struck midnight, she was on reason number fifty-seven of her third read. I was face-first and knuckle-deep in her pussy.

"Keep reading, princess," I growled, nipping her just above her pubic bone. Not hard, just enough to make her lower body jolt off the bed.

She choked back a moan. "Number fifty-seven. She's more interested in a deep conversation than small talk. Number fifty-eight."

My tongue lapped at her tangy juices before licking a line up to her clit. Her eyes drifted shut, all thoughts of the list forgotten, when I shoved a third finger inside her, stretching her nearly to her limit.

"Number fifty-eight," I prompted.

"Killian," she moaned, arching her back, fucking my fingers deeper inside her. "I can't."

"Do you need my help, princess?"

"Please."

She thrust the paper toward me, but I batted it away. I didn't need it. Not when I had committed the list to memory weeks ago.

"Number fifty-eight," I growled against her clit. I barely recognized the deep timbre of my voice.

By the time I reached sixty, she was screaming my name. By sixty-four, I was buried balls-deep inside her. And by sixty-nine (appropriately so), I had painted her tits and pussy with my cum.

After we caught our breath, I tugged her to my side, plastering her against me like a barnacle on a boat. There was nobody I'd rather drift off to sea with than the woman beside me. She rested her hand on my sweat-soaked chest. I ran my nose along the side of her head, brushing my lips over her brow.

"Happy New Year, killjoy," she said, her cheeks flushed with satisfaction, tracing a finger through the cum on her breasts.

I drew her finger to my mouth, sucking it clean. "Happy New Year, princess."

What a way to start the new year.

What a way to start the rest of our lives.

Thanks for Reading!

Thank you so much for reading *Venice Actually*!

I'll admit, when I first introduced Leighton and Killian in *Meet Me in Los Feliz*, I had no plans to write their book. I was about halfway through writing *MMILF*, when they started screaming at me, and I realized, "Crap, these two idiots are going to fall in love." And now, I love them both soooo much!

Stay tuned for Nellie's happily ever after in 2024.

If you liked this novella, please let me know and share with others by leaving a review on **Amazon** or **Goodreads :)**

Acknowledgements

Wowza. Two books in two years. I might not be the fastest writer, but I cannot believe we made it here. And I do mean *we*, because there's no way I could've made this one happen without so many people's help.

Starting with Mom & Dad. There's a hint of Wheatley in both of you, but unlike Wanda and Hank, you've always supported my choices—no matter how crazy they might seem—and encouraged me to embrace my independence. You'll never know how thankful I am for that.

Thank you to my beta, ARC, and sensitivity readers for their love and feedback. Especially, TEAM BETA – Jared, MK, Natalie, Alanna, Becky, & Laura! Your feedback never fails to make me smile, especially when you leave me suggestions for my early 2000s playlist and Angela Lansbury tidbits.

To my amazing editor, Norma, and proofreader, Valerie. Thank you both for whipping Leighton and Killian into shape (teehee, whipping) and forgiving my excessive use of ellipses.

As always, shoutout to the Bridesmaids chat, the Real Housewives of Alameda group, Wednesday & Thursday night writing groups and my Voxer Pod Squad - you all know who you are and how much you mean to me. Thank you for the hours of input, memes, incessant questions (mine, not yours) and TikTok videos.

To my pals at Daydreamer Coffee and the Sou'wester Lodge, thank you for providing me the space to work. And coffee. Copious amounts of coffee.

Finally, to Romancelandia, and to every person who has supported Boobies & Noobies over the years, thank you for welcoming me into your community. Every day, I am more and more thankful I picked up that copy of *I'm in No Mood for Love* by Rachel Gibson back in 2009. Who knows where I'd be or what I'd be doing today if I hadn't. Above all else, Boobies & Noobies has always been a podcast about exploring readers and writers' unique romance reading journeys. Thank you all for being a part of *my* romance reading journey. Hopefully, this is just the start...

About the Author

By day, Kelly Reynolds works primarily as a freelance writer, professor, and author's assistant. By night, she hosts the romance novel review podcast, Boobies & Noobies. She's ghostwritten two previous novellas, but *Meet Me in Los Feliz* is her debut self-publication.

She currently lives in Portland, Oregon. When she isn't writing, you can often find Kelly eating her way through hole-in-the-wall restaurants, sampling cider at the nearest brewery, or bingeing the latest season of "Top Chef".

Keep up with Kelly on social media @authorkellyrey and on her website: https://www.kellydaniellereynolds.com/

Keep up with Boobies & Noobies on social media and on https://boobiesandnoobies.com/

Printed in Great Britain
by Amazon